The house was silent. Standing motionless, Benny absorbed its stillness, straining for the least noise – the shift of a floor-board, the quick intake of breath – which might have betrayed Ray's presence or anyone else's. His own breathing was light and shallow, hardly lifting the rib-cage under his buttoned overcoat. But there was nothing. Even the air, disturbed by the opening of the front door, settled down again and the closed, slightly sour smell of the place reasserted itself.

Very gently, Benny lowered the zipped bag to the floor, steadying it against the side of his leg. Both hands were now free and he flexed the fingers of the right which were still cramped from holding the handle. Walking the few steps to the door on the left of the hall which stood ajar, he pushed it open with the toe of his shoe . . .

Also by June Thomson in Sphere Books:

NOT ONE OF US
A DYING FALL
SHADOW OF A DOUBT
THE DARK STREAM
TO MAKE A KILLING
NO FLOWERS, BY REQUEST

SOUND EVIDENCE

June Thomson

SPHERE BOOKS LIMITED

SPHERE BOOKS LTD

Published by the Penguin Group
27 Wrights Lane, London w8 5TZ, England
Viking Penguin Inc., 40 West 23rd Street, New York, New York 10010, USA
Penguin Books Australia Ltd, Ringwood, Victoria, Australia
Penguin Books Canada Ltd, 2801 John Street, Markham, Ontario, Canada L3R 1B4
Penguin Books (NZ) Ltd, 182–190 Wairau Road, Auckland 10, New Zealand

Penguin Books Ltd, Registered Offices: Harmondsworth, Middlesex, England

First published in Great Britain by Constable and Company Limited in 1984
Published by Sphere Books Limited in 1985
This edition 1989

1 3 5 7 9 10 8 6 4 2

Copyright © June Thomson 1984

Printed and bound in Great Britain by
Cox & Wyman Ltd, Reading

To Roy, with much love and gratitude

I

The room was exceedingly hot. The gas fire was turned on full and in front of it, stretched out on a black, half-moon heathrug, its once deep pile worn thin, lay an old, smooth-haired, brown and white terrier, as shabby and as thin-coated as the rug itself.

The dog belonged to Stanley Aspinell, one of two old men who were seated a little distance from the fire at a round table, playing chess under the light of a standard lamp which had been dragged across the room to the full extent of its flex to cast its brightness on to the chess board and pieces.

Stanley Aspinell was a small, spare, mild-looking man in his early seventies, bent across the shoulders in an apologetic stoop as if anxious to minimize as far as possible his own physical presence as he waited for his friend, Ernest Beach, to make his next move.

Beach, as befitted the owner of the chess-set and the room, not to mention the second-hand shop which opened out of it, took his time, one large, freckled hand, tufted with gingery hairs, remaining suspended for several tantalizing moments over his bishop, his bottom lip jutted out and his brow contracted with the determination to win.

A large, aggressive man, with pale, heavy cheeks which appeared to have melted and run down his face to form pendulous jowls, he sat hunched forward on his chair, huge, slack thighs hanging down over the shabby leather of its seat.

Looking round the room, as Stanley Aspinell was doing in his mild, vague way as he waited, it was possible to divine Beach's involvement with the second-hand trade. It was furnished with an extraordinary collection of objects which had either caught Beach's fancy or which over the years he had found impossible to sell and which had made their way by some strange, inexplicable process of kinesis into the small, back room. Beyond the bright circle of light cast on to the table by the standard lamp, they brooded in the shadows, impressive to Stanley Aspinell by their sheer numbers: Victorian chairs and what-nots; an elaborately carved sideboard in dark wood looking like a black, pagan altar; a chaise-longue covered in tattered horsehair; a defunct electric cooker; while the walls were so covered with prints and old, framed photographs that in places it was impossible to see the faded wallpaper behind them. But most important to Stanley Aspinell were the books. They were piled everywhere: on the chair-seats, the floor, the chaise-longue, the cooker; books which he longed to read but never quite managed to pluck up courage to ask to borrow or even to examine too closely except to squint sideways at their titles, wondering what hidden excitements *The Meaning of Treason* or the complete works of Keats might contain.

It was a treasure house to Stanley Aspinell, an Aladdin's cave of possessions which he, in his modest fashion, could never hope to own although he secretly coveted some of the items – that blue and gold plate, for instance, propped up on the sideboard or the pair of silver fish-servers next to it, displayed in their open, blue velvet-lined box; or, most especially, the picture hanging above the fireplace of a tall, fair-skinned woman, her heavy hair unbound as, gathering the folds of her long robe about her, she tentatively extended one exquisite bare foot towards a marble pool.

But for once, Stanley Aspinell's attention was not exclusively on the enamel-complexioned lady although, as he waited for Beach to make his move, his face was turned in her direction. To be exact, his thoughts were ten minutes' walk away, in a side road called Temperance Street, centred on one particular house which, for a few seconds, was so clear in his imagination that he might have been standing again on the pavement outside it as he had done earlier that evening.

The street and the house were long familiar to him. He had lived all his life in the neighbourhood and Temperance Street was one of the turnings which, as a child, he had taken on his way to school. In fact, once he had discovered the house, the road had become his favourite route.

At first sight, it seemed indistinguishable from all the others.

It was a short, narrow turning of terraced houses, their steep roofs and meagre frontages forming a brief perspective of brick and slate, broken at regular intervals by the arched entrances to passages which gave access to a narrow alleyway which ran behind the houses.

More dramatically, the house broke the vista.

It had fascinated Stanley Aspinell ever since, as a child, he had noticed the date above the door: 1912, the year of his birth. From that day onward, he had thought of it as 'his' house and had felt that their two destinies were, in some manner he couldn't explain, inextricably connected.

Its existence was not at first obvious to the casual passer-by, which added to its fascination. Half-way down the street, on the right hand side, the diminishing vista of flat façades was broken by an opening no wider than one of the passageways but, instead of a gloomy brick tunnel, a flight of six stone steps led upwards between the walls of the adjoining houses, like a narrow staircase, complete with a metal handrail and a tall, thin, iron gate which closed it off from the street. At the top, perched on a small eminence which he had never been able to decide was natural or man-made, stood the house: Holly Lodge, as an oval plaque fixed to the gate proclaimed. The holly trees in question grew at the top of the steps, one on each side, and through their interlacing branches an archway had been cut – another fascination, for it repeated in dark, glossy leaves, the arched entrances to the alleys.

After the steps and tunnel of holly, the house itself was something of a disappointment. It was smaller than might be expected, no larger than two of the terraced houses placed side by side and, like them, was constructed of dark grey brick and slate, with a central door and five sash windows, two down and three up. And yet, despite its ordinariness, it still managed to cast a spell over Stanley Aspinell. It had a closed, secretive air, as if holding itself aloof from the streets of drab little houses with their shabby corner shops and pubs, remaining untouched by the changes to which, over the years, the neighbourhood became subjected.

It was a slow process but one which Stanley Aspinell viewed

with alarm for it seemed to keep pace with his own decline into old age.

First the row of houses, known as Nelson Villas, which fronted Trafalgar Street, decent houses with their own front gardens, fell beneath the bulldozers when the road was widened, and an orange and red petrol station, neon-lit at night, took their place. Pickford Road went next and then the left-hand side of Orchard Street.

As the tide of destruction and rebuilding crept across the area, Stanley Aspinell feared for his own turning, Charlton Road, on the edge of the neighbourhood, for his pub, the Six Bells, and for the corner grocer's, now run by an Asian family, a nice enough couple although Aspinell still missed the old one-legged ex-soldier and his wife, Mr and Mrs Everett, who had been the owners when he had first moved into number seventeen as a young, married man.

It was for this house that he was particularly fearful. It was like hundreds of others, opening straight off the street into a narrow hallway where the stairs rose steeply, two rooms downstairs and three up with a single-storey scullery addition on the back and a tiny yard: cramped and inconvenient, but it was home. It was there that his three children had been born and there his wife had died. If it was pulled down, he didn't know what would become of him. He'd be rehoused, he supposed, probably in one of the new blocks of council flats. Or perhaps they'd think him past it and he'd be put into an old people's home, his greatest fear.

This was why he kept such an anxious watch on Temperance Street. It seemed next on the list for demolition. Several of the terraced cottages were already empty, their windows and doors boarded over to prevent vandals or tramps from moving in. Holly Lodge, too, seemed vacant. At least, the gate had been padlocked for several weeks and someone, presumably the landlord, had fixed a roll of barbed wire across the top.

The house had become for Stanley Aspinell a symbol of the slow, destructive process of both the neighbourhood and himself. Once that went – the iron gate, the six steps, the holly arch, the house with its mysterious air of being above and separate from the ordinary drabness of the surroundings – he knew there was no more hope for him.

And then, a miracle had happened.

Passing the house on his way to play chess with Beach that Friday evening, a weekly contest, he had noticed that the padlock and barbed wire were gone. A light glowed redly in the downstairs window to the left of the door. Someone was living there.

He had stood for several seconds in the fine drizzle of the late-October evening, his sense lifted to a height of awareness that he had not experienced since he was a child. It was as if his eyes had suddenly grown young again and he could see with renewed clarity the pavements glistening blackly in the fine rain, the wet leaves pasted flat against them, the street lamps receding in a series of moist haloes which eventually merged into one cloudy nimbus of pale light and, rising before him, the six steps, each one edged with a streak of brightness, and there, finally, beyond the dark tunnel of leaves, a rectangle of redness, like an open eye turned glowingly towards him, making him think, in a sudden rush of memories which came too quickly to be rationalized, of home and firelight and Christmas. And, above all, safety.

Everything was going to be all right, after all.

It was then, as this thought struck him and he turned away, contented and appeased, that he noticed the car parked at the kerbside. Never having owned one, he had no knowledge of its make. He only knew that it was a large, black car, probably expensive. It looked as if it had cost money and, for that reason, it seemed out of place in Temperance Street and, as he walked on towards Beach's shop, he had felt a strange disquiet, a reaction which had persisted during the rest of the evening. It overrode even the feeling of relief which the re-occupation of the house had raised in him. Something was wrong; he felt it instinctively although he could not explain it. The car was alien, discordant, symbolizing money, power and authority to which Temperance Street, with its shabby houses, did not normally aspire.

As Stanley Aspinell brooded on it, Beach at last made his move. Abandoning the bishop, he pounced instead on his knight, sending it bounding across the board in two quick decisive leaps.

'There!' Beach announced with satisfaction, as much as to say: Get yourself out of that, if you can.

Stanley Aspinell tried to concentrate his attention on the chessboard. Unlike Beach, he had never been an enthusiastic player. In fact, until Beach had taught him, he had not learnt the game and its complicated moves still confused him at times. He lacked, too, the ability to plan ahead. Beach always worked out a strategy; he even had books on chess which he studied in the slack times in the shop. He might, as he had told Stanley Aspinell, have become a county champion if he hadn't had to run a business, and Aspinell, in the uneasy alliance which formed their friendship, had believed him. Beach, intelligent and businesslike, a man of property and possessions, who put his money in the bank and owned a van, might have raised himself to any heights. Nothing was impossible.

For himself, Aspinell had no such aspirations; he knew he lacked the capacity.

Now, staring down at the chessboard, he perceived dimly that his queen was in danger. Somehow, she had to be rescued. Picking her up cautiously he moved her backwards down an open corridor of squares, Beach watching him from under tufted, sandy eyebrows with an expression of sardonic amusement.

'You don't want to have that move back again, do you?' he asked when the queen finally came to rest.

Stanley Aspinell studied the board.

His queen looked safe to him; she was flanked by two white pawns, like page-boys.

'No, I don't think so,' he replied.

Something in Beach's manner, an air of knowing triumph, stung him unexpectedly. Beach had an exasperating habit of always being right which at times roused in him an answering stubbornness, nothing very forceful, a mere mild opposition which was never voiced aloud but which was expressed in lowered eyelids and hands which linked themselves together in a gesture of quiet negation.

He clasped his hands together now on the top of his bony knees.

In the downstairs front living-room of Holly Lodge, Hugo Bannister also clasped his hands, only behind him, one inside the other, the top right hand beating a soft tattoo against the palm of the left. It was a gesture of controlled impatience and also social unease. He wanted to be gone.

The room distressed him. It was bare, ugly, comfortless, furnished merely with a folding bed, two canvas chairs and a picnic table which he had bought at a shop off Baker Street two days earlier and had transported down to the house in the back of his car. The pair of orange ready-made curtains, purchased at the same store, were fixed across the window on a length of string. The room and its contents seemed to symbolize the shifting, rootless quality of Ray's existence, living from one pay packet to the next, the future undefined, relationships formed and broken with the same lack of forethought.

He knew that he, too, would eventually be abandoned, without a backward glance, along with the room when Ray moved on.

It was part of Ray's fascination, that air of ruthless charm.

He was seated on the bed, putting on his socks, one foot cocked up, exposing a bare, soiled sole above which the two ankle bones, very white and looking oddly sacrificial, glistened in the light. The same sheen caught the top of his head, making each coarse, fair hair shine individually, and touched with brilliance the St Christopher medallion on a gold chain which had swung loose from the open neck of his shirt as he bent forward.

He was looking up, laughing, aware of Hugo's impatience and amused by it.

'Keep your hair on, Hugo,' he told him.

'I intend to,' Hugo replied stiffly, not sure if the remark was as innocent as it sounded. One never knew with Ray how much of what he said was deliberate mockery or mere friendly banter but Hugo was acutely conscious of his own thinning, dark hair, his high, bony face and etiolated body, whose elegance was almost entirely the creation of his tailor. Stripped naked, he was ashamed of it.

Ray had risen from the bed in one of his quick, supple movements and was feeling about with his stockinged feet for his shoes.

'You worry too much,' he continued. 'Do you know that?'

'Possibly,' Hugo conceded.

'You want to take it as it comes. Che bloody sera."

His face darkened as he spoke, reminded perhaps by his own words of the situation in which he found himself. There was a small silence as, finding one shoe, he crammed his foot into it, treading down the back of it as Hugo watched. He had bought Ray the shoes only six weeks ago. Hand-stitched leather, they had cost him over a hundred pounds. Already they were scuffed and worn.

Seeing them, he couldn't resist asking, 'When will your brother be coming to see you?'

'I'm not sure,' Ray replied, stamping his foot inside the shoe. His face was as sulky as a child's.

The evening was off to a bad start but Hugo lacked both the grace and the courage to retrieve it although he knew one word or gesture would have been enough. But which one? He found it impossible to decide.

It was Ray who contrived the reconciliation. As he forced his foot into the second shoe, he lost his balance and, putting out a hand, grasped Hugo's arm.

The physical contact re-established for Hugo the former intimacy between them and with it his obsession. It flowed back as palpable warmth from Ray's hand, the firm grasp of flesh which he could feel even through the sleeve of his coat. It ran through his own body like an electric charge, revitalizing it, bringing back energy to its chilly cells. Looking down on the side of Ray's bent head as he ran a finger round the back of the second shoe to ease it on, Hugo saw, as if in monstrous close-up, one neat ear, slightly pointed at the tip, clipped close to the hair-line like part of a decorative wreath, the little tuft of short, springy hair which grew beneath it and the curve of fine-pored skin above the cheekbone, faintly bloomed with the same golden light.

It was a madness, he thought. A fever in the blood. A rabies. So must Saul have felt when David first appeared before him.

At that moment, Ray looked up, the grey eyes, only a few inches from Hugo's own, bright with recognition, the pupils very large and speckled with yellow flecks like glittering seeds. The tilt of his head showed the same knowing self-assurance.

'But he'll come,' he added.

He straightened up, his hand still on Hugo's arm, maintaining the contact.

'Yeah. He could turn up anytime; perhaps tonight. You never know with Benny. But he'll see me right like you've done, Hugo. I can trust him.'

The insouciance behind the compliment, although appearing insincere, was too naïve to be anything but genuine, Hugo thought, and he accepted it as proof of Ray's desire to express his gratitude, however inept its form.

Grateful for the gratitude, Hugo said quietly, 'You know my advice, Ray.'

The young man had turned away and was putting on his coat, a zipped parka of shiny, quilted nylon. It looked new and Hugo realized, with another surge of exasperation, that some of the money he had given Ray must have been spent on clothes.

Standing with his feet apart, Ray pulled the zipper up to his neck before replying.

'Go to the police, you mean?'

'I still think it's your wisest course.'

'But I've told you already, Hugo. I can't do that. There's this mate of mine I've got to think of. He's married with a couple of kids. I can't drop him in the clag.'

It was a dialogue they had already repeated several times over the past seven days but it still reassured Hugo to hear it repeated almost word for word.

He couldn't be lying, Hugo told himself. Years of Civil Service training had taught him to be wary of the truth of any account which changed, however slightly, during repetition.

'Besides,' Ray continued, 'they'd fit me up.'

This was a new detail and Hugo demanded sharply, 'What do you mean?'

'Fit me up,' Ray repeated. 'For Christ's sake, don't tell me you haven't heard of it before? Where have you been all these years?'

'I understand the phrase perfectly well,' Hugo said stiffly, ignoring the jibing tone in Ray's voice. 'I don't see how it applies to you.'

Ray met his eyes with a candour that Hugo did not believe could be false. Surely no one, certainly not Ray, could have faked that look of clear and yet embarrassed appeal?

'Because I've got a record. Sorry, Hugo, to tell you like this. I suppose I should have come clean about it before but it didn't seem that important. It was years ago, when I was about sixteen. I was working for a bloke down in Whitechapel who had this electrical goods shop. Although I didn't know it at the time, he was handling stolen stuff – TV sets, record players, that sort of thing; had a contact in this wholesaler's, see? Anyway, he got busted.'

'And you?' Hugo heard himself asking. He was disturbed by the information, coming so late in their relationship, and suspicious of what else Ray might have chosen to conceal from him but Ray's offhand, almost negligent manner of speaking half-reassured him.

'The police couldn't prove nothing. I'd only been working there for six months but this bloke had given me a portable radio, see, which I'd got at home so they reckoned I was in on the racket. That's the way their tiny minds work. Anyway, I got probation. Funnily enough, it was the probation officer who fixed up my apprenticeship through a mate of his who ran this electrical contractor's, so in the long run it did me a bit of good.'

The conversation had drifted, as was Ray's habit, a long way from the original point and Hugo attempted to steer it back again.

'I still don't see why the police should want to fit you up, as you say, because of something that happened eight years ago.'

'Because I'm down on their books as a villain,' Ray explained with a slightly impatient air as if the reason were obvious, 'and to their way of thinking, once a villain, always a villain. So, if I go to them now and say, Look, I've been tipped off by a mate of mine that there's a mob of hard men down in Walworth who've got it in for me, first off, the Old Bill aren't likely to believe me and, even if they do, they're even less likely to do anything about it. They'll just chuck me straight back to the sharks. That's bad enough. But suppose they decide to check me out? So they start scratching around and come up with the Whitechapel records and before I know what's hit me, they've put two and two together and made not just four out of it but any bloody number they like and I find I'm booked for some job that happened, say, three years ago down in Catford or bloody Hornchurch – a wholesaler's that was done over or a factory that got busted.'

His voice had risen as he spoke, expressing a bitterness which Hugo had never heard before.

'But what about evidence . . . ?' he began.

'Don't make me laugh,' Ray replied although he smiled himself as he said it, one corner of his mouth lifting upwards in an expression of sardonic humour. 'Haven't you ever heard of evidence being planted, even prints? All they have to do is lift yours off a cup, say, on to a strip of sellotape and then roll them off on to a broken window or a blown safe at the scene of some crime. It's as easy as using bloody Letraset.'

Hugo was silent. The story which Ray had originally told him when he first came to him asking for help only a week before had now grown more complex. The first version had been complicated enough but had nevertheless possessed a straightforward narrative drive which had seemed to Hugo at the time convincing.

Ray had told him that a man he knew vaguely, a drinking companion in an East End pub, had asked Ray to join him and a group of his friends in a plan to burgle a furrier's warehouse in Stepney. Ray's firm of electrical contractors had recently overhauled the wiring and Ray, who had worked on the job, therefore had inside knowledge both of the layout of the building and the position of the alarms. Ray had not only refused but, worried about being even indirectly involved, had made an anonymous telephone call to the police, warning them of the proposed crime and its date, not knowing at that stage that a friend of his, the married man with the children, was also involved in the planned raid. In fact, it was he who had originally given Ray's name to the gang, knowing that Ray had worked in the warehouse.

Following Ray's tip-off, the police had watched the building but had bungled the affair. The same evening the crime was supposed to have taken place, Ray's friend had driven past the warehouse on a last minute reconnoitre and had seen cars parked suspiciously in the side-streets. The break-in had consequently been called off.

As Ray had said at the time, 'It was a balls-up all round.'

That hadn't been the end of it, however. The gang, suspecting Ray had tipped off the police, had decided to get their own back; quite how, Ray hadn't been sure.

'It could be anything,' Ray had said as he reached this point in the account. 'Believe me, Hugo, they're rough. They could fit me up by planting stolen stuff in the flat and then tip off the police in their turn. That's if they're feeling generous. Or they could fake a mugging. It's been known to happen. They wait for me one night and give me a going-over and, if that's what they have in mind, it could be razors and a face-job. They'd carve me up, Hugo. They wouldn't just mess about with a few broken ribs.'

As he said it, Hugo remembered Ray had run a hand over his cheeks and mouth. Above it, his eyes had the rounded, fixed look of a terrified child.

Ray's friend had warned him of the danger and Ray had moved out of the flat in Bermondsey he shared with his brother, Benny, who was away for a few days so Ray wasn't able to turn to him for help. That Friday evening, therefore, exactly a week before, he had telephoned Hugo in desperation from a public house in Fulham, one of the anonymous, out-of-the-way places where they sometimes met. Hugo had driven to the pub to pick him up.

It had been, as Hugo now saw, the first step into a morass from which he was to have difficulty in extricating himself although with the benefit of hindsight, he realized that the initial move had been made three months earlier in July when Hugo, who had wanted some new power-plugs in the flat, had telephoned a firm of electricians recommended by the porter of the apartment block where he lived and Ray had arrived, young, blithe, accommodating, singing softly to himself some vague, indistinguishable tune as, seated cross-legged on the floor, he had stripped the insulation from a length of cable.

Such songs the sirens sang.

Only, thought Hugo wryly, unlike Ulysses, he had not taken the precaution of stopping up his ears and so he had fallen victim to the enchantment.

At lunchtime, when Ray had spoken of finding a pub for sandwiches and a beer, it had been Hugo who had offered the festal banquet.

So the affair had begun with an *omelette aux fines herbes* and a bottle of Chablis '76 which Hugo had opened specially in celebration.

After that, Ray had been a regular but discreet visitor to Hugo's flat just off Baker Street, never staying the night and never taking up residence in even the most casual fashion. Hugo employed a daily cleaning-woman who arrived each morning at nine and as far as she as well as the other residents were concerned, Hugo remained the distant, aloof bachelor who appeared to have few friends.

Besides, Hugo had professional reasons for maintaining a discreet silence about his private life. As a senior Foreign Office official, he could not afford to take risks where his reputation was concerned.

He had been aware that he was being incautious when he collected Ray from the pub and took him back to the flat where, after he had sobered him up, he had listened to his story. Even then, he might have stepped back from the edge of the morass on to dry land.

It would have been easy enough, a mere matter of writing out a cheque. What would five hundred pounds or even a thousand have mattered to him in the circumstances?

Ray could then have been bundled out of his life, a room

booked for him in some hotel, a taxi called, his own telephone disconnected. Ray would have accepted it. In some ways, he half-expected it. Sitting in Hugo's drawing-room, his few possessions at his feet, he would have been willing to be bought off, and cheaply too. That was the way most of his relationships ended, Hugo imagined – casually, with no recriminations and no attempt at a reconciliation. He lacked, as Hugo had learnt during their affair, any sort of perseverance. Che bloody sera, as he himself had said.

Then why had Hugo gone to call on his cleaning-woman, putting her off coming for the rest of the week, and run a bath for Ray, instead of calling the taxi-rank?

He had considered his action many times since with the same bleak, impersonal attention with which he might have scrutinized a report submitted by a junior colleague. Here were the facts; how best might they be interpreted?

Most of it he knew already – the enchantment and the obsession – although, under normal circumstances, he would have willingly sacrificed both to rectitude. What he had not accounted for and which he found even now difficult to accept was his own sentimentality, that cheap substitute for emotion, which he had always despised. Seated on the sofa, fuddled with drink and fear, Ray had seemed as pathetic as a waif. Typically, he hadn't known what to do with his hands, clasping and unclasping them on his knees before finally, as if despairing of controlling them, he had thrust them into his armpits where he held them close.

Sentiment and pity, therefore, had played a part in his decision to let Ray remain, coupled with a curious and quite unexpected sense of moral obligation. Even as his hand went to his inside pocket for his cheque book, Hugo had been suddenly struck by the thought that all his adult life he had been paying off people like Ray; not necessarily lovers but all of those who had served him in whatever capacity: head-waiters, taxi-drivers, hotel-porters – the list was endless.

The thought had not occurred to him before and the realization disturbed him profoundly. He might have dismissed it with the excuse that this was the way in which society was organized. Why should he question it? It had served him well enough and he had no wish to see the accepted order overturned.

And yet, his hand inside his pocket, he had momentarily doubted this assumption. As an answer to a moral issue, it was too easy and for that reason was suspect. For once in his life, he felt the need not to make the obvious gesture.

So, instead of writing Ray a cheque, he had heard himself saying, 'You can stay here if you like.'

It was a decision he now bitterly regretted for it had committed himself to Ray in a way which he had not, at the time, fully realized.

However, in the first few days, he had been more concerned with the mere practicalities of sharing the apartment with someone else, especially Ray who, bored by his own company and yet frightened to leave the flat, had grown increasingly restless and irritable until on Sunday, desperate himself for a little privacy, Hugo had suggested he took him to the cottage in Suffolk. He might have guessed, however, what Ray's reaction would be. They had already spent one disastrous week there together during which they had quarrelled for the first time. Ray had hated the country. Besides, as he had pointed out, the cottage had no television set and was half a mile from the nearest pub.

'I'm not bloody well burying myself down there again, ta very much,' he had replied.

On Tuesday, there had come a reprieve. Returning from the office that evening, Hugo had found Ray jubilant. He had been in touch with his brother Benny who had returned to London and who had found a place for him to stay – in Chelmsford, in a house which was empty because it was due for demolition. Benny had arranged a short-term lease with the landlord whom he had contacted through friends. And that wasn't all. Benny was also fixing up a job for Ray in Huddersfield, only there could be a few days' delay in finalizing the details.

'So I could be off by the middle of next week,' Ray had announced.

Hugo had greeted the news with a mixture of relief and

regret. Although he would miss Ray, his departure wasn't entirely without its compensations.

Besides, he soon learnt his part in the affair was not entirely over. Ray, with a characteristic offhand cheerfulness, took it for granted that Hugo would be willing to supply furniture for the house and drive him down to Chelmsford with it the following evening.

It was suggested with Ray's usual, casual charm.

'That is if you don't mind, Hugo. Only Benny hasn't got a car at the moment so he can't help me out. Honestly, I hate asking you but I haven't got anyone else. I'll pay you back for the furniture, too, once I'm settled in the new job.'

'That doesn't matter,' Hugo had replied. 'What about the rent?'

Ray had fluttered his eyelids, a habit of his when he was embarrassed.

'Well, I didn't like to ask . . .'

'How much?' Hugo had demanded bleakly.

'Four hundred quid. I know it sounds a lot for a month's lease but it was the only place Benny could find at short notice. I'll pay you back for that as well.'

Now, watching Ray in his new, shiny parka flex his knees as he combed his hair in front of a plastic-framed mirror, also new, which was propped up on the mantelpiece, Hugo felt anger rise in him like a dark tide.

How damned stupid he'd been! If he'd given Ray a cheque for £500 at the very beginning of the whole business, he would have saved himself a great deal of time and trouble. It was a lesson to him never to indulge again in sentimentality nor to allow moral scruples to override commonsense.

Ray, his attention fixed on his own reflection in the mirror, seemed untouched by either consideration.

'Aren't you ready yet?' Hugo demanded.

The whole purpose of his calling at the house that Friday evening on his way to the cottage in Suffolk where he planned to spend the weekend was to take Ray out somewhere in the car to relieve his boredom. It was now nearly half past eight and he still wasn't ready.

'Half a tick,' Ray replied.

He was tearing the fly-leaf out of one of the cheap Western paperbacks which littered the room and scribbling down something on it, folding the sheet of paper in half so that Hugo could not see what was written on it.

On the doorstep, he bent down to tuck it under the flap of the letter-box.

'Leaving a note?' Hugo asked. 'Who for?'

Ray joined him at the top of the steps which led down to the street, pausing to draw in breaths of cold, damp air before replying.

'Oh, that,' he said casually. 'It's for Benny just in case he turns up. I said I'd be back about eleven.'

Hugo did not reply. Ray's action in leaving the note suggested that Benny was expected, another instance of Ray's lack of frankness of which Hugo was becoming increasingly suspicious.

Three days ago he might have questioned Ray, testing out the truth of what he said.

Now, getting into the driving seat and slamming the door shut, he merely asked, 'I suppose you'd like to go for a drink somewhere?'

'Magic!' Ray replied enthusiastically, wriggling his shoulders as he settled himself comfortably beside him in the Rover.

In the room behind the shop, the game of chess was over. Beach's bishop swooped forward from behind two lurking pawns and swept Stanley Aspinell's queen from the board.

'Checkmate!' Beach cried triumphantly.

As he spoke, a flurry of rain hit the window behind the closed curtains. Beach, twitching them aside, revealed a glimpse of a tiny backyard and two dustbins, their lids glistening. Already the outer glass was spattered with water-drops which were coalescing to form long, slow rivulets.

'Well, you can't go home in this,' Beach announced, making up Stanley Aspinell's mind for him. 'What about another game?'

And so it happened that Stanley Aspinell did not finally leave Beach's house until nearly a quarter to eleven, in time to witness the presence of the second car in Temperance Street.

2

It began raining before the car reached the end of the road and Hugo turned on the windscreen wipers. Through the arcs of clean glass, he could see the small, anonymous side streets, for the most part empty under the dim lighting. On the corner, noticing a public house, the Carpenters' Arms, he looked inquiringly sideways at Ray who, catching his glance, wiped the mist off the window at his side with his sleeve before leaning back.

'No, not that one, Hugo,' he said. 'I've been in there and it's half-dead. Can't we go somewhere a bit more lively? I want cheering up after being stuck in that room all this time.'

Hugo drove on without replying. Although the evidence of the new parka, not to mention the other unfamiliar objects in the room, suggested that Ray must have been out shopping in the town, it hardly seemed worth the trouble to point this out to him.

It would soon be over, he told himself. What did a few distortions of the truth matter so late in the relationship?

He was not even surprised by his own lack of response. It was a familiar absence of emotion which, until Ray's arrival, had been his natural condition, as if his feelings were withered before they were fully opened. Only Ray had succeeded in forcing them into flower, his mere presence exciting the atmosphere into bright little waves of supernormal activity to which they had leaned, like starved plants towards the sunlight.

At the next turning, he found himself in a one-way system which led him away from the centre of the town towards the outskirts. Sodium lamps glared down on wet tarmac and a row of shuttered shops, broken in the distance by the zig-zag pattern of coloured lights strung round the gables of a large public house.

'This'll do us!' Ray exclaimed eagerly. 'Slow down, Hugo.'

As Hugo drew into the car-park, Ray already had the passenger door open and was jumping out, almost before Hugo had braked, to set off at a run for the entrance, ducking through the rain and leaving Hugo to lock the doors and follow.

Entering after him, Hugo was struck by the noise and the ugliness of the place. It was like a physical assault. The one huge bar was crowded with people and crammed with patterns which met the eye wherever it turned, from the silver fleur-de-lys stamped on the maroon wall-paper to the red quilted vinyl which covered the front of the bar counter. Added to the roar of voices was the shriek of a juke-box which sent out a shattering stream of noise, indistinguishable as music apart from the heavy rhythmic beat in a lower register which seemed to vibrate through the floor and fracture the air itself.

Shouldering his way back from the bar with the drinks, he found Ray had established himself at a table which was wet with spilt beer and crowded with dirty glasses. Three other people were already seated there, a middle-aged couple and an elderly man by himself who eyed Hugo with disfavour as he approached as if his dark city clothes and silk tie were intended as deliberate insults.

'I managed to scrounge a stool for you,' Ray said, patting its seat, adding, as Hugo set his rum and coke down in front of him, 'Great! Ta very much. Cheers.'

He seemed oblivious of the silent hostility of the others seated at the table, now directed at them both. Happy and relaxed, his parka thrown open, he kept glancing about the bar, smiling to himself and beating time with one hand on his knee to the rhythm of the juke-box. Occasionally, he caught Hugo's glance and nodded to him, crinkling up his eyes to show his pleasure.

It was only when Hugo bought the second round of drinks that he spoke. Leaning forward, he beckoned with his head for Hugo to approach. As he bent towards him, Ray shouted in his ear, 'I didn't tell you but I was on the phone to Benny earlier. He says the job at Huddersfield could be sorted out by the weekend. So I could be off any time but I'll keep in touch. Promise.'

Hugo jerked his head back in order to look into Ray's face but, anticipating the movement, Ray had already turned his head away, presenting his profile only for scrutiny.

As he studied it, Hugo felt a complexity of reactions which followed so closely on one another that he was uncertain himself of their exact sequence.

So it's all finished, he thought and, almost simultaneously, He's been lying to me and, at what seemed the same time, with an overwhelming sense of relief, Thank God!

And yet, despite the confusion of his thoughts, he was able to study the side of Ray's face without any overt emotion. It was turned so far away that only the tip of his nose was visible beyond the curve of his cheek against which his eyelashes, thick and glistening, were lowered defensively as Ray studied, with apparent absorption, the glowing end of his cigarette.

Watching him, Hugo realized with the same distanced coolness, that Ray had deliberately chosen this moment to break the news to him, knowing that in the crowded bar Hugo would not be able to question him too closely or protest too openly.

Not that Hugo would have done so. He had long ago realized, almost as soon as the affair started, that it could never be permanent. Ray lacked the emotional stamina for a sustained relationship. Easily bored, he needed the constant stimulus of new lovers, new friendships, new places.

As for himself, the necessity to protect his reputation would have made it impossible for him to acknowledge openly an intimacy with any man, certainly not with Ray.

Nor did he believe in Ray's promise to keep in touch. Once he had gone, that would be the end of it and for this part of him was profoundly grateful. It had been a madness from the beginning.

All the same, as he studied Ray's profile, Hugo was aware of a sense of loss and emptiness which he could not properly define except as a yearning for something unattainable but inexpressibly precious which Ray's proximity had helped to assuage.

In the room behind the shop, the second game of chess was coming to an end. As if anticipating the home-going, the dog had roused itself and was now sitting upright on the hearthrug, exploring one ear with a tentative back paw which it scratched carefully round the delicate, pink-fleshed opening. Awake, it looked melancholy and dazed as if it had not quite recovered from the trauma of sleep, the bottoms of its eyes showing a faint rim of white. Beside it in the fender, an electric kettle was just coming to the boil.

Without thinking, Stanley Aspinell moved his castle sideways, realizing too late that it was mistake. It left his king totally unprotected.

'Checkmate!' Beach proclaimed but without his usual triumph. The game, he felt, had been thrown and he swept the pieces angrily into their box with a cupped hand.

'Well done!' Aspinell offered the congratulation as a peace-offering but it did not seem to appease Beach who stumped off into the kitchen to fetch the teapot.

Left alone, Stanley Aspinell began humming a sad little tuneless air to himself and, hearing it, the dog approached, shuffling forward with its back legs only partly raised to present its worn, grey muzzle between Aspinell's knees.

Taking it gently in his hands, he said, 'We'll be off soon, old chap. Home!'

At the familiar sound of the last word, the dog's expression brightened and its tail began to thump with pleasure against the carpet.

Over tea, which had been brewed too long and which left a metallic-flavoured fur on his teeth and tongue, Stanley Aspinell broached the subject which had been on his mind all evening, introducing it tentatively for, although he was anxious for Beach's opinion, he was unsure of his reaction.

'You know that house in Temperance Street . . .' he began.

'What house?' Beach demanded.

'The one standing by itself with the steps up to it.'

Even then, Aspinell could not bring himself to speak its name for fear that, in doing so, he might cause bad luck either to it or to himself.

'Yes, I know the one you mean. What of it?'

'Someone's moved in there.'

'Who?'

'I don't know,' Stanley Aspinell admitted, beginning to regret having spoken. 'There was a light on in one of the downstairs rooms when I came past this evening.'

Contrary to his expectations, Beach looked interested.

'Are you sure? Only I know for a fact the whole of that street's due for redevelopment.'

Beach always knew the facts of any topic that might be under discussion.

'Well, there was a light,' Stanley Aspinell repeated with a touch of his former stubbornness, 'so someone must have moved in.'

'Squatters,' Beach asserted, as if that were the end of it.

'I don't think so,' Aspinell replied, remembering the car he had seen parked outside. For much the same reason that he had not named the house, he did not like to speak of having seen it. It would be like trying to describe a nameless fear.

'Someone from the council then, looking the place over. An assessor. Bound to be.'

Stanley Aspinell wasn't sure what an assessor was so he kept silent while Beach, despite his conviction, hastened to shift the subject to more certain ground.

'That whole street's due to come down in the spring. The council's only waiting to rehouse the rest of the tenants and then they'll take over. I wouldn't be surprised if they don't start on this street next.'

'But what about your shop!' Stanley Aspinell cried. In his concern for his own future, it had not crossed his mind that Beach's could also be in jeopardy. He had always seemed unchangeable, like a rock or a tree, rooted in this one place, buttressed against the forces of decay by the sheer weight of his possessions.

Beach shoved out his lower lip.

'Can't say it bothers me,' he replied with an air of massive indifference. 'They'll have to pay me compensation. The shop's a going concern so I'll get a good price for it. If I don't, there'll be trouble, I can tell you. I was thinking of retiring anyway. What with the compensation and my savings, I reckon I could set myself up in a little bungalow somewhere by the sea. I've always fancied the seaside.'

It was a long speech for Beach to make and, as he listened to it, it occurred to Stanley Aspinell that Beach was trying to impress himself as much as anybody else. He, too, was afraid and this realization added to Aspinell's own sense of unease.

Putting down his empty cup, he fetched his coat from the hook behind the door and put it on, carefully wrapping his scarf first round his neck.

'I think I ought to be going, Ernest. Thanks very much for the tea and the chess.'

'You want to practise more,' Beach told him. 'You'll never make a chess-player if you don't study the moves. I'll lend you a book on the game.'

Before Stanley Aspinell could protest, Beach had hauled himself to his feet and, lumbering across the room, had picked out a thin volume from the pile on top of the cooker. Thrusting it into Aspinell's hands, he added, 'There you are. You read that before next Friday. I want it back, mind.'

Aspinell looked at the torn grey cover on which the title *Chess for Enthusiasts* was printed above a black silhouette of a knight. Below it in an empty space, stamped in bright blue ink, were the words 'E. Beach, Secondhand Dealer, 54 Thackeray Street'. All the books in Beach's shop were marked in this manner. It discouraged, Beach said, his customers from pilfering them.

'Thanks very much, Ernest,' Aspinell said brightly, trying to look pleased as he slipped it into his raincoat pocket. He wondered if it might be a good opportunity to ask if he might borrow something else more to his own taste but before he could pluck up the courage, Beach had opened the door into the shop and was turning on one of the naked electric light bulbs.

In the dim lighting, the interior looked menacing. Stanley Aspinell had never felt comfortable in it, especially at night. Now, remembering Beach's words about its possible demolition, it seemed to him that the process had already begun. The piled-up furniture had the appearance of barricades or the aftermath of some wholesale rampage by looters who had gathered together the spoils of conquest in one great heap before dividing it out between themselves. There was a strange smell, too, about the place which disturbed him, an old, sad smell of worn upholstery and carpets which seemed to him redolent of loss and decay.

It would not have surprised him on stepping into the road to find Thackeray Street in ruins, the bricks tumbled down on to the pavements and the sky lurid with flames.

But, as Beach opened the shop door, Stanley Aspinell found that nothing had changed. There was the street, the houses, the pavements, looking drenched and subdued after the rain and the only light in the sky was the red glare cast up by the orange standards on the new one-way system in Nelson Street.

'See you next Friday then, Ernest,' Stanley Aspinell said.

Beach nodded.

'And thank you again for the book.'

But Beach appeared not to hear him. He had shut the door and was reaching upwards to push the top bolt into position.

Turning away, the dog at his heels, Stanley Aspinell set off for home.

At the same time that Stanley Aspinell was putting on his coat, Hugo also decided to leave. Touching Ray briefly on the arm to attract his attention, he pointed wordlessly at his watch at which Ray, slipping his arms into his parka, rose and followed him out of the bar.

In the car, they maintained the same silence. Hugo had already made up his mind to say nothing to Ray about his departure. The onus, he felt, was not on him, although from time to time he glanced sideways at Ray as if inviting some comment, but his face, caught in the passing light of the street lamps, was closed and sulky.

It was only when they turned into Temperance Street that he spoke at all.

'You're not angry with me, Hugo?' he asked.

'No, why should I be?' Hugo replied, trying to make his voice sound indifferent.

'Only you've not said much all evening.'

'There didn't seem much to say.'

Which was the truth. There was either nothing to talk about or too much and at that late stage in the relationship it seemed pointless to begin.

'Are you all right for money?' he added. There seemed little else left that he could offer.

'Well, I am a bit short,' Ray admitted.

Hugo drew the car into the kerb outside the house and, leaving the engine running, felt in his inner pocket for his wallet, drawing out some notes which he passed to Ray.

'There's fifty there,' he said. 'It should keep you going until you're settled in your new job.'

'Thanks.' Ray sounded subdued as he stuffed the money into his pocket. Removing his hand, he laid it on Hugo's knee. 'Hugo,' he continued, 'I can't tell you how much . . .'

'Then don't try,' Hugo said. In the light from the dashboard, he could see Ray's fingers spread out on the dark cloth of his trousers and he looked down at them quite objectively as if they were unconnected to himself although the warmth of the contact was an entirely personal sensation.

'I'll write,' Ray promised.

The next moment, he was scrambling out of the car and was passing in front of the bonnet where he was brilliantly spot-lit for a few seconds in the headlights, one hand grasping the neck of the parka which glistened as if it were wringing wet.

Then he passed out of the brightness into the shadows of the street as, shouldering open the gate, he disappeared up the steps.

Hugo put the car into gear and drew away slowly from the kerb. As he did so, its lights swept across the façade of the house, picking out a second figure which at that moment emerged from the porch to greet Ray who, out of sight under the holly arch, was still approaching the door.

Hugo had only a brief glimpse of the man: a narrow, pale face and dark hair which fitted close to the scalp and came down low over the ears in long sideburns, giving the odd impression that he was wearing a black bathing cap pulled down close about his head.

The next second, the car had passed the house and the man was no longer visible.

Hugo had no doubt who he was. It was Benny, Ray's brother, although having now seen him Hugo doubted the relationship. There was too much dissimilarity in their appearances. He was also convinced that the visit had been planned. The note which Ray had tucked into the letter-box seemed to confirm it.

It didn't matter, he told himself. It's all over. The lies, the deceit aren't important any more. Forget them. Forget him.

Intent on these thoughts, he noticed neither the elderly man with the dog who was walking down Temperance Street nor the car parked a little distance away on the opposite side of the road.

Stanley Aspinell, however, was more observant.

He was approaching Holly Lodge from the Trafalgar Street end and was in time to witness the car draw up and a young man get out. He recognized the car as the same one he had seen earlier parked outside the house when he had passed it on his way to Beach's. The man was unfamiliar.

Aspinell was walking slowly for the sake of the dog which padded stiffly at his heels and he was too far away to see the man's features, although, as he crossed to the pavement in front of the headlights, Aspinell had the impression that he was young, fair-haired and was dressed in a short blue coat, like a windcheater.

The next moment, he had pushed open the gate to Holly Lodge and disappeared up the steps. At the same time, the car drove away.

Stanley Aspinell was disappointed. He would have liked to observe the new occupant of the house at closer quarters but, by the time he drew level with the gate, the front door was closed and there was nothing to see except the hall light shining through the coloured glass of the transom.

All the same, he lingered, waiting for the light to be switched on in the downstairs room. Shortly afterwards, he was rewarded. The darkened oblong to the left of the door suddenly glowed orange and Stanley Aspinell, satisfied and comforted, walked on.

As he did so, he was aware for the first time of the second car, dark blue in colour, parked a little distance down the road and facing towards him. Although its headlights were switched off and it appeared empty, he realized, as he drew nearer, that someone was seated in the driver's seat. A pale blur of a face was just visible through the windscreen.

Anxious that his interest in the house might appear suspicious, Aspinell glanced towards it as he passed and was aware that the man seated inside it was also looking in his direction.

If he had been asked, Stanley Aspinell could have supplied a description of the man, so clearly was that one brief moment of contact stamped on his memory before, embarrassed, he turned away, pretending to call the dog which plodded at his heels.

'Nearly home, old boy,' he told it.

A few minutes later, he had reached the end of the road and turned right into Argylle Street.

Inside Holly Lodge, Ray led the way into the downstairs front room, peeling off his coat and throwing it down on the bed.

Behind him, Benny was asking, 'Who was the geezer in the car then?'

'That friend of mine I was telling you about,' Ray replied.

'Not old Huggy Bear?'

It was a nickname which Benny had thought up when Ray had first mentioned Hugo's name, amused by what to him were its classy overtones, a version Ray had thought funny at the time. Tonight, subdued by the coolness of Hugo's departure which he regarded as a form of rejection, he merely replied sulkily, 'He's all right.'

'I never said he wasn't,' Benny countered. 'I just think you were stupid to involve him. The fewer the people in the know the better.'

'What else could I do?' Ray protested. 'You'd gone pissing off down to Brighton with that new boy friend . . .'

'So I had!' Benny seemed pleased to be reminded.

'Make much out of it?' Ray asked. He was curious to know as well as anxious to change the subject.

'Not bad. Apart from the money and five days in the best hotel, I got this.'

Shooting out his wrist, he displayed a watch on a broad, gold strap.

'Christ!' Ray said admiringly. 'You know how to pick 'em. All I got was a week down in bloody Suffolk and a few clothes.'

'So how much does he know?' Benny demanded, reverting to the original subject.

As they had been speaking, he had been inspecting the room, walking about with a lounging negligence and picking up Ray's possessions to examine more closely. In the harsh light of the unshaded bulb, his face seemed composed of sharp points and hollows, his hair as lustrous as leather.

Ray, who had crossed the room to light the gas fire, squatted in front of it, rubbing his hands and holding them out towards the bars as he watched Benny's movements warily over one shoulder.

'Who?' he asked.

'Huggy Bear, who the hell else should I mean?'

'Nothing about the Hampstead job, I swear it. I told you, I pitched him a yarn.'

'Which he swallowed?'

'Yes, although he'd heard of the break-in; it'd been on the news. As a matter of fact, he mentioned it. The job I told him about was down in Stepney. He didn't make the connection.'

'It's happening all the time,' Benny remarked vaguely. He had wandered over to the bed where he picked up Ray's parka, running a hand down the sleeve. 'This is new, isn't it? Been out shopping?'

Still squatting, Ray turned on his heels to watch Benny's movements.

'Only a couple of times. There was stuff I needed.'

'Anywhere else?'

'Down the fish and chippie.'

Abandoning the parka, Benny picked up instead one of the Western paperbacks and smiled as he turned over the pages as if he found the contents secretly amusing.

'What about this evening?' he asked casually.

'Hugo took me out for a drink.'

Benny's reaction was as rapid and frightening as a snake suddenly rearing its head and striking.

Throwing the paperback book down, he swung round on his heel.

'You went out for a bloody *drink*! For God's sake, what do you think you're playing at?'

Ray crouched back as if avoiding a physical blow.

'It was Hugo's idea,' he began.

'I don't care whose stupid idea it was. You should have known better. Where did you go?'

'Some pub on the outskirts of the town. Honest, Benny, it was packed out. No one noticed me.'

'That's what you think. Let's hope to Christ you're right.'

'But they won't be looking for me down here,' Ray protested. 'They don't even know I was on that job.'

'Don't they? They'll be looking for you bloody everywhere after tonight.'

'Why?' Ray asked. He got to his feet and stood in front of the fire, arms straight by his sides as if to attention.

Benny grinned at him.

'Because, you stupid prat, they've picked up Webber. The word was out this evening before I left to come here.'

'Webber won't say nothing,' Ray began.

'Won't he? He'll drop you and Garston straight in it,' Benny replied, his smile broadening. 'Don't you listen to the radio?'

Ray glanced fearfully at the portable set standing on the mantelpiece as if its very presence there was reassuring.

'I listened to the one o'clock news,' he explained.

'What about this evening's?'

'I – I was asleep earlier . . .'

'You were having a bloody kip!' Benny seemed to find this information even more amusing. 'And then I suppose lover-boy turned up and you didn't bother listening in after that?'

Ray didn't reply although the quick, nervous fluttering of his eyelids confirmed that this was, in fact, what had happened.

'So you didn't happen to hear that the policeman Garston smashed has copped it?'

'Copped it?' Ray repeated stupidly as if the words had no meaning for him.

'Yes, you cretin, bloody bought it. "Died without regaining consciousness", as the news put it. So it's a full-scale murder inquiry from now on and, knowing Webber, he'll fall over himself to point the finger at somebody else.'

As he said it, he pointed his own finger at Ray who stared at it as if down the barrel of a gun.

'Sweet Jesus!' he said softly.

'Now you see,' Benny continued with the jaunty air of having been proved right, 'why it wasn't very clever of you to go pissing off to some pub or even down the fish and chip shop, especially wearing that thing.' Picking up the light blue parka, he shook it contemptuously. 'Look at it for God's sake! It's like bloody fluorescent lighting.'

'I'll get rid of it,' Ray said quickly.

'Too bloody right you will. In fact, you'll get rid of the whole frigging lot. Dump it somewhere. And do something about your hair while you're at it.'

'My hair?' Ray asked, running a hand over it.

'Dye it; shave it off; anything. I don't give a toss. But get it done before Monday when you leave for Liverpool. Or were you thinking of catching the train from Euston looking like that?'

'I hadn't thought . . .' Ray confessed.

'God, you're still wet behind the ears, aren't you? Do I always have to do your thinking for you?'

'I didn't know it'd be like this,' Ray protested, his voice rising. 'How was I to know Garston'd clobber that copper? He said no rough stuff. I thought it'd be a push-over . . .'

'Then you don't know Garston, do you? You want to pick your friends more carefully.'

'Yeah,' Ray agreed in a subdued voice before adding, 'You got the papers, Benny?'

'They're here,' Benny replied. Feeling in his overcoat pocket, he produced an envelope which he handed to Ray. 'And don't bloody lose it. There's a National Insurance card in there, plus a driving licence, both made out to Desmond O'Brien. In other words, you're a Mick from now on.'

'Where did you get them from?' Ray asked, examining the contents of the envelope eagerly.

'Never you mind. Let's say Mr O'Brien's found it more convenient to leave for the Emerald Isle under another name.'

'They won't get me into trouble?' Ray asked fearfully.

'Not unless you fancy going into the bomb-making business. No, straight up,' Benny added, catching sight of Ray's expression, 'you'll be all right if you keep your nose clean. There's a single ticket to Liverpool in there as well for the 2.15 on Monday so make sure you're bloody on it. You'll have to sort out somewhere to live for yourself when you get there.'

'Yeah, I will. Thanks very much,' Ray replied. He propped the envelope up behind the radio before continuing, 'What about my gear, Benny? I mean, I'd better not go out to the shops myself tomorrow, had I?'

Benny lifted his shoulders, expressing long-sufferance.

'All right; I'll get the stuff for you if you'll give me the money. I'm short at the moment. And I'll buy a bottle of hair-dye at the same time. How do you fancy yourself – as a blonde or a redhead? Better make it dark brown, though; you don't want to stand out from the crowd. If I can find a shop selling theatrical gear, I'll get you a false moustache or a pair of glasses; something that'll alter your appearance. As for clothes . . .'

'I'll leave that to you, Benny,' Ray put in, anxious to please. 'Anything'll do. I can always kit myself out again when I'm up in Liverpool. How much are you going to need?'

Benny thought briefly.

'Three hundred quid ought to do it.'

'Three hundred! But I've already given you a thousand for the papers!'

'There's the train ticket, not to mention the hotel.'

'What bloody hotel?'

'The one I'm going to have to stay in tonight or do you suggest I kip down here on the floor? I'm certainly not bunking in with you in that folding contraption over there,' Benny replied, indicating the camp bed.

'All right,' Ray agreed sullenly. 'Hang on here a minute. I'll have to fetch it.'

As the door closed behind him, a curious stillness came over Benny in contrast to the restlessness he had shown earlier. Standing motionless and expressionless in the centre of the room, his face turned towards the ceiling, he listened intently as Ray's footsteps echoed up the uncarpeted stairs. At the top, they paused and there was the sound of a door opening before they continued across the floor of the room immediately above. Benny counted them silently. At five, they stopped again although Benny could hear the faint vibration through the plaster of the ceiling as if someone were pressing back with his heels against the floorboards immediately in front of the chimney breast. It was followed by the grate of metal on stone and then, quite distinctly, two sharp little clicks as if a suitcase had been opened. There was silence for a few seconds and then the sequence of sounds were repeated in reverse order. By the time the footsteps descended the stairs and Ray re-entered the room, Benny was propped up against the mantelpiece, idly turning over the pages of the Western paperback which he had retrieved from the bed.

'There's the money,' Ray announced, handing over a bundle of notes. 'Do you want to count it?'

'I don't think so,' Benny replied lightly. 'If you can't trust a friend, who's left to rely on?' Folding back his overcoat, he tucked the money into his jacket pocket, adding, 'I'll be off then. See you tomorrow about eleven.'

Ray followed him into the hall where he opened the door. Stepping into the porch, Benny paused, turning towards him and patting the side of his face with one hand.

'Bye-bye, sunshine,' he remarked. 'And keep your pecker up, as the actress said to the bishop.'

Above the sharp cheekbones, his eyes glittered with suppressed laughter. The next moment, he had gone, walking with an air of nonchalant self-assurance towards the holly arch.

Behind him, Ray slammed the door shut and leaned against it, his arms folded against his chest as if in self-protection, his expression sombre, before returning to the living-room where he kicked off his shoes and, lighting a cigarette, lay down on the bed, staring bleakly at the opposite wall.

A few minutes later, there was the sound of a double knock at the front door.

'Piss off, Benny!' Ray called out. 'You're getting no more frigging money out of me.'

All the same, he rolled off the bed and, laying the cigarette on the edge of the mantelpiece, padded into the hall in his stockinged feet.

'What's the matter with you then?' he added as he opened the door. 'Fancy bunking in with me after all?'

3

At half past ten the following morning, Hugo locked the door of the cottage and set off up the lane in the opposite direction from the small cluster of houses and the one shop which constituted the village.

It had been a mistake to come here, he decided. There was too much about the place which reminded him of Ray – an absurd concept because Ray had been essentially a creature of the city. Nevertheless, it was here that they had spent the week together that Hugo had intended as a country idyll, and everywhere he looked there was something, no matter how mundane or trivial, which contained recollections of Ray and of his own high hopes.

It hadn't, of course, worked out that way. Closing the gate behind him, Hugo remembered, with that selective process of recall which filters out the dross and leaves only the clear, pure essence of memories, not the anger or the frustration but the moments of reconciliation, the lamplight falling on Ray's shoulders and the scent of vanilla which seemed to exude from his skin and hair.

Even his feeling of relief at Ray's departure which had sustained him the previous evening was superseded by a sense of pain and loss which he knew nothing would appease, while that rational part of his mind which yesterday had enabled him to observe Ray's deception with such cool objectivity now failed to comfort him.

Stepping out of the shelter of the garden, he realized that the wind had risen. As he walked, he could feel it pushing against his back, like a huge hand, propelling him along. Overhead thin, grey clouds, torn into tatters, raced along just above the treetops, looking like smoke driven from some monstrous conflagration. The wind was almost a visible presence. Dark and furious as an avenging spirit, it buffeted the trees, snatching down the leaves which scudded in front of it along the lane in frantic retreat as it hissed and seethed in the dried mounds of last year's dead bracken along the verges.

This was how the world would end, Hugo thought, in a tumult of noise and angry dissolution.

As he topped the rise, the landscape emerged from behind the hedges, curiously static after the ferment of the nearer view. Beneath a sky of dark, layered grey, the countryside lay sullen, pieced together with trees and hedges picked down to the bone by the wind which seemed to have scoured the whole countryside clean so that it lay empty before him, a patched vista of ploughland and fallow, some fields still blackened where the stubble had been burnt after the harvest.

He had walked this way with Ray, he remembered. They had stopped here at this same gateway to look across the Stour valley to the view that Constable would have known.

But how different it had been then! Soft, rounded, enclosed in foliage, it had seemed richly contented, bright under the clear East Anglian light which, even in the height of summer, still contained that hard, sea-brilliance which enabled the eye to travel for miles to the far, blue distances where the clouds repeated in their own skyscapes the same rich fullness of the fields.

He liked to think he had been contented then, a mood which, as he rested his arms along the top bar of the gate and stared bleakly at the autumn landscape, he preferred to recollect rather than yesterday's parting when Ray had passed momentarily in front of the dazzle of light from the car's headlights, leaving behind a brief after-image which was less permanent than its accompanying sense of loss and betrayal.

Stanley Aspinell did not notice the sky as he went out into the backyard to empty the bag of rubbish into the dustbin. Unless it were raining or snowing, it rarely impinged on his consciousness. It was merely a small, irregular, empty rectangle between the surrounding rooftops and chimneys. He noticed, however, the drift of white petals which had blown against the shed door where the wind had stripped the last rose from the climber which, crucified on wires, was nailed back to the wall and, pinching them up between his fingers, he sniffed at them to catch their last fragrance before consigning them to the bin along with the empty dog-food tin and the ball of concentrated fluff from the vacuum cleaner.

The tin reminded him that he would need to go to the corner shop to buy more for the weekend – one of liver, one of beef, he decided, checking the label on the discarded tin which had 'Rabbit' written on it over the picture of an alert-looking spaniel, bright-eyed and glossy-eared. Like an elderly invalid, his own dog's appetite needed cosseting: a little of this, a morsel of that, never the same flavour two days running.

'Fussy, that's what you are,' Stanley Aspinell would tell it, not without a touch of pride.

He'd go after his midday meal, he thought. The outing would help break up the afternoon. Since his retirement, and especially since the death of his wife five years before, he had found time more and more unwieldy. It stretched out before him in a long ribbon of days and weeks and years which he could only adequately manage by snipping into smaller portions.

And while he was out, he could easily walk round to Temperance Street to look at the house in daylight and see if he could catch a glimpse of the new occupant.

He did not expect the cars would still be there. In the mundane light of Saturday morning, the menace they had seemed to suggest had faded, although he still remembered the embarrassment he had felt when he had passed the second car and seen the man looking at him.

Well, he wouldn't loiter outside the house this time. He'd simply walk past it quite naturally, just glancing up the steps towards the front door. There'd be no light on, of course, but

41

there might be other signs of occupation – smoke from the chimney or an empty milk bottle on the door-step.

Then home by way of Argylle Street in time for tea and a wash and change because that evening his son-in-law would be calling for him to baby-sit while he and his wife, Aspinell's youngest daughter Marilyn, went to the pictures together.

Satisfied that he had the rest of the day nicely portioned out, Stanley Aspinell replaced the lid of the dustbin and re-entered the house.

Benny turned into Temperance Street, walking quickly, anxious to get inside the house out of the wind and to relieve himself of the hold-all he was carrying which contained the stuff he had bought for Ray that morning. Its handle cut into his palm and prevented him from putting that hand into his pocket. The knuckles felt seared by the cold.

All the same, it had been worth it. The clothes and the bottle of hair-dye hadn't amounted to more than sixty quid which left him over £200 to the good. The spectacles had cost him nothing. He'd nicked them out of a box in a charity shop where he'd bought Ray's tweed jacket: some appeal on behalf of short-sighted Pakis. Trying them on later in the lavatory of the café he'd gone to for a cup of tea, it had been as much as he could do to refrain from laughing aloud at his own reflection and the distortion which the lenses added to it.

Well, Ray would have to lump it, he thought. It was all his own bloody stupid fault anyway. I hope they give him migraine.

The curtains of the downstairs room were still drawn, he noticed as he climbed the steps. Ray was probably having a lie-in and, annoyed at the delay this would cause before the door was opened, Benny banged hard on the knocker before leaning across to tap on the window.

When, after a few moments' delay, no one came, he squatted down in front of the door and, pushing open the letter-box, called down the hall, 'Come on, Ray! Let's be having you!'

There was no answering shout from Ray and no sign of him when, squatting further back on his heels, Benny looked through the slit in the door. The narrow opening revealed nothing except a glimpse of stairs rising to his left and, beyond them, through an open doorway, the edge of a white porcelain sink and a wooden draining board.

Straightening up, Benny stood for a moment in thought and then, going to the bottom of the steps, glanced quickly up and down the street. Apart from a milk-float, trundling along in the middle distance, it was deserted.

Satisfied, he returned to the porch where he leaned against the wall as if waiting for someone to answer his knock. At the same time, he took his wallet out of his inside pocket and, having extracted his cheque card from it, tested its flexibility against his thumb before inserting it into the crack between the door and jamb.

The door was badly fitting and the plastic oblong slid easily down the crack until it came to the tongue of the lock. Having located its position, Benny did not even bother to observe what he was doing. With his face turned towards the window and his left hand plunged deep in his overcoat pocket, the action of his right hand was concealed even from himself although he felt the card flex in his palm as he worked it to and fro until at last he felt it slip past the flange, easing it back into the lock. Removing his right hand from his pocket, Benny rested the tips of his fingers against the door which yielded softly under the pressure. With one last, swift glance at the small portion of the street visible below the holly arch to reassure himself that it was empty, Benny stepped quickly over the threshold and closed the door after him.

The house was silent. Standing motionless, Benny absorbed its stillness, straining for the least noise – the shift of a floor-board, the quick intake of breath – which might have betrayed Ray's presence or anyone else's. His own breathing was light and shallow, hardly lifting the rib-cage under his buttoned overcoat. But there was nothing. Even the air, disturbed by the opening of the front door, settled down again and the closed, slightly sour smell of the place re-asserted itself.

Very gently, Benny lowered the zipped bag to the floor, steadying it against the side of his leg. Both hands were now free and he flexed the fingers of the right which were still cramped from holding the handle. Walking the few steps to the door on the left of the hall which stood ajar, he pushed it open with the toe of his shoe.

It swung back, releasing a blast of warmth. Beyond the room lay half-submerged in a subdued orange twilight, caused partly by the daylight straining in through the curtains and partly by the glowing bars of the gas fire which was still burning in the hearth.

In front of it, lit richly by its reflection, Ray lay sprawled out on the worn lino as if asleep, his legs drawn up and his head resting on a dark pillow which had spread out under his hair.

Feet apart, Benny stood looking down on him with an expression of alert, fastidious curiosity. He had seen a dead man only once before but he had no difficulty in recognizing death in Ray's face. He was struck most of all by the stupidity of features, the looseness of the mouth which had fallen open a little and the eyes which were staring with a look of fixed vacuity at a pair of shoes which lay discarded by the bed a few feet away as if, at the moment of dying, he had been trying to puzzle out what they were doing there.

Squatting down by the side of the body, his hands on his knees to maintain his balance, Benny followed the unfocused stare to the shoes and then up to the bed, across the bottom of which Ray's blue parka was still lying where he had discarded it the night before. From there, his eyes travelled round the rest of the room, marking the position of the objects it contained and plotting each move he would have to make.

Before rising to his feet, he turned back to Ray's body, and brushed the top of his hair briefly with the tips of his fingers, while avoiding the shattered side of his skull. It was warm from the fire and felt strangely alive. As he lifted his hand, he saw the thick strands, disturbed by the contact, spring back into place.

It was the only farewell he could bring himself to make. He did not like to touch the rest of the body. The flesh already had the static look of death. But he felt some gesture was called for, however slight, in token of – what? He himself wasn't sure. Not love. Then comradeship, perhaps. Something, anyway, that had been shared between them and that demanded a sign of recognition from the living to the dead.

That done, he rose to his feet and crossed the room to carry out the actions he had already planned.

First the parka. Lifting it by the collar, he went swiftly through the pockets, finding and removing the fifty pounds in tenners which were folded across the middle into a thick wad. He thumbed through them before transferring them to his own pocket. The envelope containing the papers and the train ticket was still propped up behind the radio and he checked its contents before thrusting that away inside his wallet.

He moved quickly and lightly in the half-light, balancing on the balls of his feet like a dancer as he crossed and recrossed the room, repeating the series of movements he had made the previous evening as he wiped with his handkerchief every surface he had touched, even the front and back covers of the Western paperback which he remembered handling.

Next the door. Even though Ray had opened it when they had entered the room together the previous evening and he had not touched it that morning, he rubbed the edges and the handle inside and out.

Better safe than sorry, he thought.

In the doorway, he paused to look back at Ray, curled up in the orange twilight. For a moment his expression softened, the hard, tight angles of the features relaxing before, turning his back, he retreated into the hall.

The stairs protested gently as he mounted them, and he trod carefully, keeping to the centre of each tread between the metal clips which had once held a carpet in position, his arms by his side, touching neither the rail nor the wall.

At the top, a narrow landing ran towards the back of the house, lighted only by the panels of frosted glass in a door at the far end which led, he assumed, into a bathroom. The door on his left was closed.

Wrapping the handkerchief over his hand, Benny turned the handle and entered. The room beyond was empty. Flowered wallpaper, swollen with damp, had eased itself from the plaster in places and bellied forwards, the pattern washed pale. On his right, an egg-shaped light switch in brown bakelite dangled from the ceiling at the end of a long flex where presumably a bed had once stood and an old gas fire, its frets broken, stood on a hearth of white glazed tiles facing him.

Benny took five steps forward. He was now standing in front of the fireplace, its narrow cream-painted mantelshelf gritty with old dust which held the clear imprint of fingers as if someone, before bending down, had gripped the edge to steady himself.

Taking care not to touch the mantelpiece himself, Benny crouched in front of it. The gas fire, he noticed, had been disconnected. The pipe, emerging from a hole in the floorboards at the side of the hearth was capped off and the hardboard blocking the opening, into which the gas fire had been inserted, was broken along the edges. The dust which lay on the tiles was also disturbed. Two narrow paths had been cut through it below which the surface of the tiles was scored with long scratches.

With the handkerchief still covering his hand, Benny inserted his fingers under the fire and pulled it forward. It moved slowly, catching on the hardboard, its feet grating on the hearth. Behind it lay a cavity, filthy with soot and brick dust which had dropped down the chimney but empty apart from an oblong indentation stamped into the grit where something heavy had been standing. The case had gone.

Benny crouched back on his heels. The angles of his face hardening.

He was too bloody late. The same sod who had murdered Ray must have got him to admit where the case was hidden before bashing the side of his head in. It wouldn't have been difficult. Ray was a frigging coward where violence was concerned. You'd only got to show him a fist or a knife and he'd be down on his bloody knees.

He straightened up, wiping his hands on the handkerchief and brushing off the dust from the knees of his own trousers. It was time to clear out.

Downstairs in the hall, he paused only to pick up the zipped bag and wipe his prints from the inside of the front door and then, without a second glance at the room where Ray's body was lying, he let himself out of the house, checking his watch as he did so.

The whole business hadn't taken much more than seven minutes, he reckoned.

The street was still empty apart from the milk-float which had now reached the far end.

Turning in the opposite direction, Benny walked briskly away towards the station.

He had quarter of an hour before the next train to London, time enough to make a 999 call from the public phone box on the forecourt before he bought himself a ticket and mounted the steps to the platform.

Detective Chief Inspector Finch stood hump-shouldered at the window of his office, looking down moodily at the tops of the cars drawn up at the traffic lights in the road below and wondering what the hell he would say to Boyce, his Sergeant, when he arrived.

Something would have to be said. He couldn't allow the situation to drag on indefinitely. All the same, he was exasperated by the necessity. It was so damned childish.

The plain fact of the matter was Boyce was jealous and the cause lay in a set of circumstances for which no one was to blame except the Sergeant himself.

Two months earlier, a new Detective Sergeant, Colin Munro, had joined them from the Chelsea force, an experienced officer who was good at his job.

At first Boyce had taken to Munro, initiating him into the district and passing on to him the kind of information that a man, newly arrived in an area, might have taken weeks to find out for himself. Boyce had even, or so Finch understood, introduced him to his favourite pubs and treated him to drinks in off-duty hours.

With hindsight, Finch could see there had been an air of patronage about Boyce's friendship with Munro, the slightly superior attitude of the experienced towards the uninitiated which in Munro's case hadn't been justified. He might be younger than Boyce; he might be unfamiliar with the patch; but he was no fool and he learned quickly. Boyce's period of tutelage had consequently been short and before long it had become apparent that Munro no longer needed his services as mentor, a situation which Boyce had resented.

Matters had come to a head when Boyce had been away with flu for a week. In his absence, a case of arson on a farm had cropped up, not a big inquiry and one that had soon been solved. But, with Boyce away on sick leave, Finch had taken Munro on to the investigation, finding him efficient, alert and, moreover, intelligent. They had worked well together, a situation which Boyce on his return to duty, hadn't found at all to his liking.

In other words, his nose had been put out of joint. As a result, an uncomfortable atmosphere had developed which even Finch, isolated in his office, had become aware of. Boyce now avoided Munro whenever he could, sniffed disparagingly whenever his name was mentioned and found as many opportunities as he could to make some slighting reference to new brooms sweeping clean or people not knowing their place. It had all the makings of an ultimate show-down.

In some ways, Finch could sympathize with Boyce's feelings. In the years they had worked together, they had built up a good professional relationship which the Sergeant must resent being disrupted. He thought, quite wrongly, of course, that his position as Finch's right-hand man had been usurped by an outsider. But even while sympathizing with him, the Detective Inspector felt exasperated.

For God's sake, their relationship wasn't exclusive! Besides, what else could he have done under the circumstances? He had needed a reliable Detective Sergeant; Munro had fitted the bill. Finch had no complaints about him except he had a tendency to be a little too pushy. But he was young and he was obviously keen on promotion; he wasn't the type to hide his light under a bushel, and provided he didn't overstep the mark, which so far he hadn't done, Finch was willing to welcome him on to the team.

But it had to be a team and Finch was not prepared to allow

petty jealousies on the part of Boyce or anyone else to spoil the effectiveness of the group of men who worked under him.

Besides, he had personal considerations on his mind which added a sense of frustration to the mounting professional pressures and which he found more difficult to view with the same dispassionate judgement.

In fact, although he had tried to push the problem out of his thoughts, it still remained a source of irritation because of the very uncertainty of his own reactions.

Was he in love?

It seemed a ridiculous question for anyone to ask himself, certainly a middle-aged Detective Inspector of Police. Falling in love was something that either happened or didn't; or so one was led to believe by the contemporary sub-culture of popular songs and literature. One was not supposed to be in doubt about it.

In love.

Standing at the window, Finch considered the phrase. He had always associated it with a relaxed and comfortable condition, like getting into a warm bath at the end of a long, tiring day; not exactly high romance but he was objective enough about himself to realize that he was not built for passion and that his stocky frame and broad, bluff features hardly suited the conventional image of the lover.

It was part of his dilemma; he simply could not envisage himself in the role. The absurdity of it struck him as soon as he considered his own reactions.

And yet, behind the familiarity of his own self-image, Marion Greave's still rose to disconcert him.

Pardoe had introduced him to her only a week before as his replacement as police surgeon while Pardoe himself was on leave and, although that initial meeting, which had taken place prosaically enough here in Finch's office, had only lasted at most about ten minutes, it had been long enough to disturb the Chief Inspector's normal equanimity.

Small, dark, quiet, Marion Greave, who was in her late twenties or early thirties, could not be considered pretty or even attractive in the normally accepted meaning of the term. To use

Boyce's words when summing up women of his acquaintance, she was 'nothing to write home about'.

It had been Finch's own reaction as he shook hands with her although, at the time, he had been struck by an air of self-possession about her and the firm grasp of her hand as it had lain briefly in his, as well as the tiny crinkles of skin under her eyes which gave her whole face an amused look which was appealing.

It was only when she moved away to sit down on the other side of the desk that he had noticed the poise of her head and the steady gaze of her dark eyes as she regarded him. The realization that she was quietly summing him up had been a new and uncomfortable sensation.

He was willing to admit that he had also been disturbed by the thought that he might have to work with her as a colleague. Although he had no strong feelings either way about women's liberation, he was prepared to concede that his attitude was based entirely on the fact that he had never yet been required to work with a woman on a basis of professional equality. There were women police officers, of course; it wasn't an entirely masculine world he inhabited but they did not offer any real competition.

Marion Greave, he felt, had.

He remembered thinking at the time that, with a little luck, any cases that turned up in the next three weeks during Pardoe's absence wouldn't include sudden or violent death. There would then be no need for him to become involved with her and he could put her out of his mind.

But it was easier said than done and he had become increasingly exasperated by his inability to control his own thoughts which had developed the habit of sneaking off unbidden to contemplate a wide-browed face, a pair of dark eyes and, what was more important, a still centre into which he caught himself gazing as if into a woodland pool or the heart of a flower.

It was absurd! The very images themselves were ridiculous.

Consequently, he was in no mood to deal calmly with any other emotional problems which Boyce might present him with. He had quite enough already on his plate, thank you very much.

All the same, as Boyce knocked and entered the room, he felt a twinge of pity for the burly Sergeant. He looked far from well although Finch suspected that the lugubrious expression and the hacking cough which Boyce managed to produce the moment he crossed the threshold were exaggerated in order to rouse his own guilt and sympathy.

'You sent for me, sir?' Boyce asked, coming to attention at the far side of the desk with a long-suffering expression which said all too clearly, I don't know why I've been sent for but, whatever it is, I'm bound to get the blame.

'Ah, Tom!' Finch exclaimed in a voice which to his own ears was much too bright and welcoming. 'It's about this report of Wylie's. I'd like you opinion . . .'

He had the folder already on his desk: a mere sop, as he himself was prepared to admit, the sugar on the pill to make the real purpose of the interview more palatable.

He was ashamed of himself at having recourse to such a subterfuge and ashamed, too, for Boyce's sake when the Sergeant's hangdog expression lifted at the remark.

In the event, however, the folder proved unnecessary for, as Finch stretched across the desk to get it, the telephone rang and he picked it up instead, listening impassively to the message which was conveyed.

As he replaced the receiver, he was aware of Boyce's curiosity which seemed to come across as little eager waves like those from a dog which, before anything has been said, anticipates an outing.

'That was a report on an anonymous 999 call,' Finch said. 'You'd better round up the others. A dead man's been found in a house in Temperance Street.'

'Murder?' asked Boyce at the door. His voice had a husky quality about it but whether from excitement or the after-effects of the flu Finch did not bother to consider as he grabbed up his mackintosh and followed Boyce out into the corridor.

'God knows,' Finch replied.

As he said it, his mind was on other matters. Firstly, he still hadn't done anything positive about Boyce and Munro who would now be working together on a major investigation. That was bad enough. To add to it was the uncomfortable realization that Marion Greave would form part of the same team.

4

On arriving at the house in Temperance Street, Finch was grateful that he was almost able to forget her in the first flurry of activity.

The room where the body was lying was small and the dead man occupied most of the space in front of a gas fire which was still burning in the hearth. As he stooped over him to make his first brief examination, Finch noted the wound behind the left ear and the blood which had disfigured that side of his features so that, looking down at him as he lay slumped on the floor, he saw only the travesty of a human face.

At that early stage of the inquiry, the examination was cursory, forming only a part of his general observation of the whole scene although he had already reached one conclusion as he straightened up.

It was almost certainly murder. He couldn't see how such a wound could be self-inflicted or accidental. Having come to that decision, he stepped back from the body as if deliberately distancing himself physically from it, absorbing certain details about it and the room in which it was lying with a few, rapid glances, storing away the first vital impressions for later consideration.

The photographs which McCallum, the police photographer, was already taking would remind him later of the disposition of the body and its surroundings but they could not re-establish the special atmosphere which every scene of crime possessed nor his own immediate reaction to it.

The body was of a young man in his mid-twenties, fair-haired, good-looking. At least he had been. The unspoiled right-hand profile which Finch observed as he stepped across his legs to view the body from another angle showed clear-cut features, a good line to the nose and chin with full, well-modelled lips. The clothing he was wearing didn't give much away: jeans and a blue and white checked shirt which could have belonged to a lorry-driver or a student although the Western paperbacks which Finch had noticed lying about suggested that the dead man's literary taste hadn't been exactly high-brow. A pair of good quality leather shoes were discarded by the bed, unpolished like his own, the back trampled down. In comparison, the parka lying across the foot of the bed looked flash: too much white piping on the pockets and round the collar and one of those wide-toothed white plastic zips running up the front.

The room was square, papered with the sort of abstract pattern in coloured rectangles which had been popular in the sixties – pop art for the masses – while the furniture, a folding table and a couple of chairs, was of the type that you would take on a picnic in the boot of a car. They looked new. So did the bed. That also could be folded down but it had a more substantial metal frame with a thin foam mattress laid over rubber stretchers. It stood in the right-hand chimney alcove, facing the door, its head pushed up against the wall, the pillow propped up lengthways. A navy-blue sleeping bag lay on the top of the mattress.

The room was now filling up with the experts. Besides McCallum, Wylie, the scenes of crime officer, and the two fingerprint specialists had crowded into the confined space and Finch had to squeeze past them as he made his way across the room towards the bed, anxious to confirm an impression before he bowed out and left them to their work.

It was as he had thought. Both the pillow and the sleeping-bag looked as if someone had been lying there, head and shoulders against the pillow, torso and legs stretched out on top of the bag. He could see the clear impression of the body.

From there his glance travelled down again to the shoes lying beside the bed on the shabby lino and from them upwards to the mantelshelf immediately above the bed-head where a cigarette had burnt itself out. The charred paper tube was still sticking to the softened paint while below it, on the green tiles of the hearth, a long roll of ash had fallen.

It would appear that someone, presumably the dead man, had been lying propped up on the bed, his shoes off and smoking a cigarette which he had placed on the mantelpiece before getting up.

Finch glanced back at the body. Wylie would check the pillow for hairs, of course, and forensic would run a saliva test on the cigarette which would confirm or deny the assumption, although it seemed plausible.

What had happened next was pure conjecture.

Had he got up to let the murderer in or had the killer already been in the room with him?

There seemed no way of discovering the answers to these questions although Finch was convinced that the victim and the murderer had known each other which would narrow down the field of suspects once they had established the identity of the dead man. All the evidence pointed that way. There was no sign of a forcible entry. The front door had been shut, the back door not only locked but bolted. All the windows were intact, their latches fastened. In fact, in order to enter the house, Finch had had to send one of the young Detective Constables, Kyle, to break in by a downstairs window at the rear of the building.

Nor was there any indication of a fight or a struggle in the room. The victim had been killed with one savage blow to the side of the head; and it had happened, Finch estimated, some hours ago. The drawn curtains, the fire and the one bare electric light bulb still burning in the room suggested the murder had taken place at night, either after dark the previous evening or in the early hours of the morning. The doctor would be able to confirm the time of death and, as the thought occurred to him, Finch remembered with an unfamiliar lurch of the heart that it would be not Pardoe, but Marion Greave.

He turned abruptly from his contemplation of the bed, thrusting aside her small, cool image, to concentrate instead on a last swift appraisal of the room and the body it contained.

What the hell had he been doing here in the first place? The minimal furnishings suggested a temporary occupation but, all the same, Finch did not think he had been a squatter. Squatters do not usually move in off the street with new furniture nor a front door key, and one lay on the mantelpiece next to a portable radio, a battered luggage label attached to it with the address written on it in worn ink. It looked like the sort of key a landlord might hand over to a tenant.

Well, that was one fact which could be established without too much difficulty and he tramped out of the room to find Kyle whom he despatched to the Rates Office to discover the name and address of the owner of the house. Boyce had already been allocated to search the upstairs rooms with a small group of men. Standing in the hall as Kyle departed, Finch could hear their footsteps echoing across bare floorboards on the first floor, the noise punctuated at regular intervals by the sound of Boyce's cough.

Perhaps he hadn't been exaggerating after all.

Munro and another team of detectives were searching the downstairs rooms and the garden.

As he had divided out the tasks, it had seemed a good idea to separate the two Sergeants, making them responsible for their own particular part of the investigation, although Finch realized that he was merely postponing a problem which sooner or later would have to be tackled head on. At the thought, he felt overwhelmed by a feeling of exasperated unwillingness which robbed him of that high sense of anticipation which normally preceded a murder investigation. The hunt was up but, instead of the thrill of the chase, he felt like one of those followers-on-foot who plod wearily along in the rear, a reluctant participant in the excitement.

He'd get over it, of course. He'd have to. There was a job of work to be done and if that meant a confrontation with Boyce and a second meeting with Marion Greave, so be it.

Shoulders humped, he moved towards the kitchen.

He had already made a brief tour of the house on arrival, opening doors and sticking his head quickly round them as he established the lay-out.

All the rooms were empty apart from lino on the floors and a few fitments and were of mean proportions as if whoever had designed the building had limited himself to the minimal requirements, although the house itself was something of an oddity, perched up above the level of the terraced cottages which surrounded it, as Finch had observed when he had first approached it up the steps which led under a holly arch. Isolated, too – an impression which was confirmed as he checked the view through the windows. Although it might be possible to overlook the upstairs windows from the opposite houses or catch a glimpse of the façade from the narrow view afforded up the steps, the back of the house was completely sheltered by high brick walls which surrounded the garden. There was no back entrance either as Finch discovered for himself, ambling out, hands in pockets, to survey the rear elevation. The garden ended with the blank wall of a builder's yard in the next street. Anyone entering the house would have to come up the steps to the front door.

The line of policemen searching the garden were almost certainly wasting their time, Finch thought, as he stood for a moment watching their inch by inch progress through the tangle of overgrown plants, bushes and grass of what had once been lawn, shrubs and flower-beds. All the same, he nodded to them encouragingly before returning to the kitchen where Munro was squatting down over a cardboard box containing rubbish which he was painstakingly sorting through.

As he shut the door behind him, Finch heard a woman's voice in the hall and recognized it instantly as Marion Greave's. Wylie must have let her in for Finch heard him say, 'Through here, doctor.'

He was showing her into the front room where the body was lying.

Her arrival placed Finch in a dilemma. With Pardoe, he would have known exactly how to react. Without giving the matter a second thought, he would have walked into the room, greeted Pardoe and stood watching while the police surgeon began his examination.

Now, he felt absurdly uncertain. To appear too quickly

might seem over eager. To wait too long, off-hand and negligent. Besides, what on earth should he say to her?

As he hesitated, Munro said, 'Someone's been down the fish and-chip shop a few times.'

He was picking greasy papers from the cardboard box and putting them aside in a separate pile.

Glad of an excuse to linger, Finch said, 'Probably the victim. It doesn't look as if he did much cooking.'

As he spoke, he glanced about the kitchen at the stained sink and the old gas-cooker, its white enamel top blackened with patches of burnt-on grease. Apart from a cheap tin kettle, a mug, a plate and some cutlery, there were no other utensils in the place. A jar of coffee granules, a bag of sugar and a half-empty carton of milk stood on a shelf above the draining-board. The man had evidently been camping out in the house and this, too, suggested a temporary occupation.

'Had quite a few beers, too,' Munro added, indicating the collection of empty lager tins he had assembled on the floor.

He stood up, flexing his knees and grimacing. Upright, he was a tall man, taller than Boyce but not so broad-shouldered; in his mid-thirties, or so his official papers stated although Finch realized that, in fact, he knew very little about Munro's personal background. Unlike Boyce, he never chatted about himself. He was a bachelor; this much, too, Finch had learned from his papers although what he did in his off-duty hours, the Chief Inspector had no idea. Did he have a girlfriend? He certainly appeared to have made no close friends among his colleagues apart from a mere day-to-day professional contact, and Finch had the impression that he was something of a loner who had little need of other people's company – perhaps, indeed, despised it. A self-contained man. The phrase seemed to sum him up. Also a little hard. Ruthless, even, with that single-minded drive of a man who does not intend remaining at the bottom of the heap for long.

It was an impression which was apparent in his physical appearance. The thick, dark moustache he sported gave him a middle-aged look and added to his features a certain positive air which was emphasized by heavy eyebrows and full, moist, brown eyes which at times had the disconcerting habit of remaining fixed on the person he was talking to with very little movement of the lids. There was the same assertiveness in his manner of speech which he'd be wise to learn to modify for some of his superiors if he wanted to get on. Although Finch didn't personally object to it, he could see that Munro might give the impression of too challenging an attitude.

Boyce had said that he was a bit too damn cocksure and, to give Tom his due, he was right in some ways. But Munro's self-assurance was not entirely misplaced. The man was alert and intelligent, more intelligent probably than Boyce himself, and Finch suspected that this was a large part of the trouble. Boyce might have more experience but it was men like Munro who got to the top. They were bright, ambitious, prepared to work hard, not just at the scene of a crime but over the paper-work as well. Boyce lacked that attention to detail. He was good at his job but with a stubborn, plodding perseverance. Although in Finch's opinion neither man had much imagination, Munro possessed a quality which almost amounted to perception: an active mind that was able to draw deductions quickly from a set of facts.

As if to prove this point, Munro said, indicating the pile of papers, 'I could get one of the DC's to check at the local fish-and-chip shop, sir. I noticed there was one on the way here, on the corner of Trafalgar Street. It might give us some idea of his movements.'

With an amused exasperation, Finch noted the use of the pronoun 'us' which could suggest that Munro considered himself on an equal footing with a Detective Chief Inspector and he felt momentarily in sympathy with Boyce's attitude to the man.

Yes, Boyce was right; Munro could be pushy.

On the other hand, he might simply be identifying himself with the team and, if that interpretation were correct, it was entirely laudable.

All the same, he felt it necessary to put Munro in his place, however pleasantly.

'When you're through with the search here, you can send

Marsh to make inquiries but I don't want anyone taken off the team yet.'

To give Munro his due, he accepted the mild rebuke with no outward sign of resentment. Stiffening into an attitude of attention, he replied, 'Very good, sir,' with the correct air of formality which Finch in his turn acknowledged with a slight, formal inclination of the head before walking out into the hall.

However, pausing outside the door which led into the front room, his self-assurance faltered. Faced with the imminent second meeting with Marion Greave, he realized he had no recognized pattern of behaviour on which to rely, not even a sense of the superiority of rank to give him confidence. There was nothing he could do except plunge in and hope to God that he didn't make a mess of it by saying the wrong thing or appearing too eager to please: or by going to the other extreme, too unfriendly. It was a delicate balance which he was not sure he could maintain and he had the uncomfortable feeling that, whatever attitude he chose to adopt, Marion Greave with her cool intelligence would probably see through it.

The door was ajar and he pushed it open boldly. After all, he had every right to be there.

The scene inside the room should have been familiar to him. Many times during his career, he had witnessed a police surgeon examining a body and had stood by watching with an aloof objectivity, although in some cases, particularly those involving children or young people, he had never quite learned to control the overwhelming sense of compassion for the victim and the sense of the futile and terrible waste of life. Besides, in most inquiries, Pardoe had acted as police surgeon and his matter-of-fact presence had helped him preserve that unemotional approach to violent death.

Now, standing in the doorway, he was unprepared for his own reaction to the sight of Marion Greave kneeling by the body. She had taken off her outdoor clothes and put on a white overall-coat and surgical gloves. An opened bag of instruments stood beside her on the hideous mock-parquet lino.

For a moment, she was unaware of his arrival, intent on examining the wound above the dead man's ear, her fingers lifting aside the thick hair, clotted with blood, to expose the shattered skull.

For the first time for years, Finch felt revulsion rise in him in a nauseous tide.

He couldn't be sick, he told himself. Not in front of her. Nor in front of Wylie and the others either. Christ, what a fool he'd look!

Swallowing hard, he stepped forward, making his presence known, acutely aware of the shabby, unprepossessing figure he must present.

She glanced up and smiled pleasantly enough in a brief acknowledgement of their acquaintance – nothing special about it, though, Finch noticed with a sense of unwarranted disappointment. God knows what he had been expecting.

'Murder?' he asked, trying to make his voice match her smile.

'I don't think there's any doubt about that,' she replied. 'That blow couldn't have been self-inflicted and it's unlikely that it was accidental.'

'There's nothing in the room to suggest it was,' Finch replied and realized, as he spoke, that he had blown it. In his anxiety, the statement had come out too brusquely as if he intended putting her in her place by showing off his own professional expertise. He saw the corners of her lips straighten. Hastening to retrieve the situation, he continued, 'I mean, there's no evidence that he fell and struck his head.'

With one hand he indicated the flimsy furniture in the room.

'Of course,' she said dismissively as if that much were obvious and, turning away, resumed her examination of the body.

Stuffing his hands into his pockets, Finch edged past her and went to stand by the fireplace where he had a view of her back in its virginal white overall and her bent head. From that angle, she appeared like a woman at prayer, kneeling submissively. Her hair, he noticed for the first time, was cut short and curled about her head in dark, glossy tendrils which reminded him of ivy leaves.

He felt absurdly *de trop* and uncomfortably aware of the

others in the room: Wylie who was painstakingly picking hairs from the pillow with a pair of tweezers and dropping them into an envelope, and Marsh and Hunt who were checking the furniture for fingerprints. They too seemed ill at ease. There was none of the usual banter between them, as if the presence of a woman in the room had put them, like small boys at a grown-up party, on their best behaviour.

Finch cleared his throat before addressing the back of her head.

'Any idea how it happened?'

She didn't even bother to turn round.

'I can't be sure at this stage but it seems probable that he was struck from the front, almost certainly by a man or a strongly-built woman. It was a savage blow and he must have died instantly. As for the weapon . . .'

'We've found nothing,' Finch put in too quickly. 'The killer must have taken it away with him.'

'I can't tell you much about that either at the moment,' she continued, ignoring the interruption. 'There's nothing in the wound that I can see – no splinters of wood, for example – but I may be able to give you more details on that when I put in my report.'

Her voice had a clipped quality, almost man-to-man in its cool professionalism.

'Time of death?' Finch asked, managing at last to match his tone to hers.

He was rewarded by the glance she gave him over her shoulder, amused and yet at the same time acknowledging his keenness.

'I was just about to take the rectal temperature.' As she spoke, she was briskly unzipping the man's flies and pulling the jeans down over the hips. 'If you could help me turn the body over,' she added.

As Finch stooped to help her, grasping the man under the shoulders, he was in closer proximity to her than he had ever been before. He could see the fine line of her brows and the thick, short lashes which gave the edges of her eyes a fascinatingly furred appearance.

Not much make-up, he noticed, observing her with her own professional coolness which he surprised himself by being able to maintain despite her physical nearness. A hint of powder blooming the cheeks which had an attractive upward sweep to them, the lips only slightly reddened. It was a face, he decided, which was best seen at close quarters. At a distance, its planes, her most attractive feature, lost their distinctiveness and she became merely ordinary, her appeal resting almost entirely in her personality and the cool, slightly astringent quality she conveyed.

He could even smell it about her: an antiseptic freshness which all doctors seem to exude, but behind that he could detect a more spicy perfume, perhaps from the scent she used, which was entirely her own.

'Over!' she said and he was ridiculously pleased that they worked in synchronization. Lifting the body together, they turned it over on to its face.

Finch stood up. Mercifully, the wound was no longer visible apart from one blood-stained wing of hair. But he was disturbed by the sight of the man's buttocks emerging from the top of the jeans and by Marion Greave's small, firm hands as they pulled the trousers further down to expose them fully.

Boyce's arrival couldn't have been better timed. Putting his head round the door, he asked in a plaintive voice as if expecting to be rebuffed, 'If you could spare a moment, sir?'

Glad of the reprieve, Finch followed him out into the hall.

'Yes, what is it, Tom?'

'We've found something upstairs that I'd like you to have a look at.'

As they entered the bedroom immediately above the room where the body was lying, Boyce added, 'I haven't moved it yet. I thought McCallum should photograph it first and it ought to be fingerprinted.'

He was indicating a gas fire which was fitted into a small, cream-painted fireplace in the wall directly opposite the door.

'See those scratches on the tiles and the way the dust's been disturbed?' Boyce continued. 'Someone's pulled the fire forward. There's a set of prints, too, on the mantelshelf.'

All this Finch could see for himself but he repressed any exasperation he felt at Boyce's tendency to state the obvious.

Striding back on to the landing, he shouted over the banisters for McCallum and Hunt to come upstairs.

When the police photographer had taken his shots of the gas fire *in situ* and Hunt had dusted it for prints, Boyce eased it gently forward and, squatting side by side, Finch and the Sergeant peered together into the cavity behind.

I hope to God he doesn't say something's been standing there, Finch thought, observing the oblong indentation in the dust.

But to his relief, Boyce merely remarked, 'I'll get that photographed and measured. Could have been an attaché case,' he added, standing up and coughing behind his hand at the small dust grains which the removal of the fire had released into the air. 'It's the right shape.'

'Or a box,' Finch put in. 'Containing what, though? Papers? Money? Jewellery? Something anyway that someone wanted kept hidden.'

Presumably the dead man downstairs. Perhaps that was why he had been killed. The murderer had wanted possession of whatever had been concealed behind the gas fire. It could provide a motive, although he realized it was too early in the investigation to jump to that conclusion.

Stepping back, he gave McCallum room to set up his camera to photograph the inside of the cavity.

'Found anything else?' he asked Boyce.

'No,' the Sergeant replied. 'We've gone over the other rooms and they've been fingerprinted but there's no sign any of them have been used except the bathroom. There's a roll of loo paper in there and some shaving gear. The geyser's been lit, too. Seems he must have washed in there but didn't bother to take a bath – at least, not judging by the dust in it.'

Finch confirmed this for himself before returning downstairs.

In the hall, he checked his watch. It was now half past one and he tramped back into the kitchen where Munro was packing up the rubbish into plastic bags. The search of the garden had been completed, too, and the men were standing about in small groups, waiting for the next assignment.

A break for lunch seemed indicated and he despatched those men who were free to the nearest public house, the Carpenters' Arms, for sandwiches.

Returning to the hall, he was in time to meet Marion Greave emerging from the front room. She had changed back into her outdoor clothes, a dark tweed overcoat cut on cossack lines with a high fur collar out of which her small head emerged like a flower. She looked much more feminine although her voice still contained the same brisk tone.

'I've finished with the body for the time being if you want it moved. I'll get a report to you as soon as possible when I've done a more detailed examination. I'll also give you an estimated time of death at the same time.'

'Thank you, Dr Greave,' Finch replied. It was the first time that day he had used her name, he realized, or her professional title.

She held out a small, gloved hand to him. He shook it more firmly than was strictly necessary, trying to express God knows what, and he saw the little pouches under her eyes crinkle up with amusement as she smiled back at him, adding to his confusion.

In awkward haste, he circled round her to open the front door and stood watching as she walked down the short path to the steps where her figure, upright and trim, descended. Beyond, he caught a glimpse of the crowd which had gathered round the gate, faces turned upwards towards the house. A uniformed constable shouldered a pathway for her and she passed out of sight.

Retreating inside the house, Finch closed the door.

They might meet again, perhaps in connection with her report; he didn't know. All he was sure of was his own uncertainty regarding his feelings towards her which this second encounter had done nothing to resolve.

5

'Come on, out you go!' Stanley Aspinell commanded with mock severity, holding open the front door.

Showing the whites of its eyes in a long-suffering expression, the dog plodded reluctantly over the threshold on to the pavement. As he shut the front door after it, Stanley Aspinell realized that the apparently calm weather of his small, sheltered backyard was not repeated here in the open street. A brisk, cold wind blew down the narrow road, as through a funnel, bowling along empty crisp packets and even a discarded beer can which rattled down the gutter until it lodged in the gridding of a drain where it rocked backwards and forwards a few times before finally coming to rest.

With the dog's lead looped over his wrist, Stanley Aspinell hastened to button up his raincoat, realizing as he drew the edges together that the book on chess which Ernest Beach had presented him with the previous evening was still in the pocket.

It was hardly worth the trouble to find the front door key and enter the house to leave it on the hallstand. The book was too small to be an inconvenience although, as he twitched the lead to galvanize the dog into action, he could feel it bumping gently against his right thigh as he started off down the street.

He already had his route planned out. Left at the end into Argylle Street and then left again into Temperance Street which would take him past Holly Lodge where he could use the book as an excuse to stop outside the house by transferring it from one pocket to the other. He could then take a good look at the place without appearing to do so. Later, on the way back, he would call at the corner shop which he still thought of as Everett's, despite the change of ownership, to buy the tins of dog food and a small loaf. This would save him having to carry the shopping further than was necessary. As he grew older, these small conservations of energy became important. Then home to watch television before getting ready for his son-in-law's visit and an evening spent baby-sitting at Marilyn's house.

Turning into Temperance Street, he was surprised to see several cars parked along the road and a crowd of some twenty or more people gathered on the pavement. At that distance, it was impossible to decide exactly which house they were congregating in front of, although he was aware of a special quality about their stance and grouping which reminded him of wartime. People had stood about in much the same manner on the day the bomb dropped on Becket Street demolishing two houses and part of the public house, the King William. On that occasion, too, women had clustered together, coats thrown hastily over shoulders, some still wearing aprons and slippers, and had leaned towards one another in the same attitudes of shocked but fascinated distress.

Something terrible had happened, that much was obvious, and Stanley Aspinell faltered, reluctant to proceed and yet urged on by an overwhelming need to know, for it was now quite apparent to him that the focus of their horrified interest was Holly Lodge. As he hesitated, a man emerged from the opening where the tall, iron gate stood and pushed his way through the crowd. At the same time, the top of a policeman's helmet suddenly became visible above the ranks of heads and shoulders as a uniformed officer moved forward to clear a path. The man, young and wearing civilian clothes – Marsh, in fact, despatched by Munro to make inquiries at the fish-and-chip shop in Trafalgar Street – walked briskly towards one of the parked cars and, slamming the door, drove off down the road. There was a sense of urgency and purpose in his sudden departure.

'What's happened?' Stanley Aspinell asked tentatively, approaching the crowd and addressing the backs of those nearest to him. He was on the edge of the group and could not see the house itself, only an oblique view of the narrow opening between the surrounding terraced cottages where the steps rose steeply.

A woman turned, her mouth twisted into a conventional tragic shape, the lips pinched and tight.

'There's been a murder.'

She dropped her voice on the last word as if she were reluctantly mouthing some obscenity.

'Murder?' Stanley Aspinell repeated the word too loudly. Other heads turned. Shocked faces looked towards him. He was an interloper who had broken the taboo which bound them together in a decent, low-keyed appreciation of sudden, violent death.

Their reaction embarrassed him. Suddenly and unexpectedly, he stood out from the crowd, a position which he had spent most of his life actively avoiding. Under normal circumstances, he would have backed away apologetically but the memory of the young man he had seen passing so briefly in front of the car headlights gave him a new boldness and persistence.

'Whose?' he demanded.

The woman turned back again and looked him up and down dismissively, establishing the fact that he wasn't a resident in the street and was therefore, as an outsider, entitled to only the minimum information.

'I don't know. That young bloke who was living there, I suppose. Don't ask me.'

She presented her back to him again in a decisive manner, quite clearly indicating that she had no intention of speaking to him again, an attitude which she further emphasized by entering into a low-toned conversation with the woman standing next to her, effectively shutting him out.

Stanley Aspinell turned away, hauling at the lead to encourage the dog to its feet. During the exchange, it had sat down on the pavement, its shoulders drooping as if it bore the whole weight of canine misery.

Walking more rapidly than usual, Stanley Aspinell retraced his steps to the corner of Argylle Street where he stopped, aware by the tightening of the lead that the dog was having difficulty in keeping up with him. It had broken into an awkward, shambling trot, its tongue lolling from side to side. A long string of saliva drooled from the corner of its mouth.

'Sorry, old chap,' Stanley Aspinell said gently, pausing to wipe his eyes. He had been facing the wind which had stung them, making them water. Fumbling in his raincoat pocket, he found his handkerchief and wiped them carefully, dabbing finally at the end of his nose where he felt a water drop gathering.

What a pair we must look! he thought. Anyone would think I was crying. As for the dog, it had sat down again, panting heavily, the saliva drops making dark stains on the paving stones.

Casting a quick glance back at the crowd to see if anyone had witnessed their discomfiture, he saw that no one was showing the least interest in them. All eyes were turned towards the house.

Now that he had halted, he had time to consider what he had been told.

Murder!

The word had always seemed to him ugly, whether printed in a newspaper headline or spoken on a news bulletin. It possessed a death-like knell in the two heavy syllables which reminded him of the tolling of a bell. He seemed to hear its sonorous, double chime ringing out now above the clamour of the other thoughts and images which crowded into his mind as he stood wiping his eyes and nose, as if foretelling the doom not only of the house where the murder had taken place but his own.

But, despite the confusion, he had no doubt that the body lying inside Holly Lodge was that of the young man whom he had glimpsed so briefly the night before. Indeed, his sudden passing in and out of the lights seemed to Stanley Aspinell in retrospect to possess a significance far above normal, casual observation. It was as if he had been fated to witness that short, transient passage from darkness into the light and then out again into the shadows, and he could recall quite clearly, as if the figure had been branded on to his retina with some fiery substance, the light blue jacket and the thick, fair hair over which the brilliance of the headlights seemed to gather as in the haloed pictures of saints.

It was absurd, of course. Even he recognized the extravagance of the image just as he knew that, in recalling the other face he had glimpsed behind the windscreen of the parked car, he was dramatizing the pallor of the features and the air of watchful menace which the man had seemed to convey.

All the same, someone ought to be told. The police, he supposed, and, remembering the uniformed policeman on duty at the gate, he half-turned towards the crowd. But a reluctance to break through their ranks and thrust himself forward in so positive a manner made him hesitate.

Divisional police headquarters were only a short walk away. It might be better to go there and pass on the information in a more private manner. That way, if he had made a mistake and his evidence was worthless, he wouldn't look too much of a fool in front of others.

The desk constable, a plump-faced, young-looking uniformed officer in his late twenties, glanced up from a report he was reading to watch the elderly man cross the open space in front of the building and mount the steps to the glass doors.

Reaching them, the man seemed to have second thoughts, for he paused to peer inside before slowly tugging open the door and entering, an old, shabby dog at his heels.

The constable was in two minds about their arrival. Since the earlier excitement when Finch and the other detectives had departed on the murder case in Temperance Street, not much had happened and he was half-inclined to welcome any diversion. The man looked decent enough, too: a quiet, respectable type.

On the other hand, the constable had settled down into a quiet routine of doing nothing very much and he doubted if the old man would come up with anything exciting. He wasn't too sure about the dog either. It looked old: the sort that might make puddles on the polished floor.

'Yes?' he asked impassively, eyeing them both up and down as they approached the desk, establishing his authority on the far side of the counter.

'I'd like to speak to someone in charge,' the old man said. He looked flustered and the colour had risen in his cheeks, but the constable could detect behind his nervousness a tremulous defiance.

Oh, God, he's one of those, he thought and pressed his chin

down firmly against his collar. Someone's nicked a pint of milk off his doorstep and he wants to see the Super about it.

'Well, I'm in charge at the moment, sir,' he replied, making his voice sound pleasantly jocular. 'Won't I do?'

Stanley Aspinell was aware of his patronizing tone and resented it as he had done Beach's superiority. He could always walk away, of course, but having come so far, it seemed stupid to back down. Clasping his hands together on top of the counter, he said, 'It's about what's happened in that house in Temperance Street.'

He was gratified to see the constable's expression change to one of genuine interest.

'You mean the murder inquiry, sir?' he asked.

'That's right,' Stanley Aspinell replied, pleased that it was the constable who had voiced the word 'murder' rather than himself. 'I think I might know something about it.'

'I could take down any details.' The constable reached for a pen and a notebook. 'Your name and address, sir?'

'No.' Stanley Aspinell spoke with unexpected firmness. 'I want to speak to whoever's in charge of the case.'

It wasn't exactly stubbornness which had led him to this decision, although he still felt offended by the constable's manner. Besides, the man seemed so young: not the sort of person he wanted to confide in. Unsure himself of the importance of what he had seen, he feared that the constable might further belittle it out of inexperience or through that air of false geniality of the young towards the old. Stanley Aspinell was afraid of being made to look a fool.

The constable looked disappointed.

'Detective Chief Inspector Finch is in charge of the inquiry,' he replied. 'He's at the house now . . .'

'I've just come from there,' Stanley Aspinell put in, anxious lest the constable might suggest he returned there. 'There's a crowd of people outside. I'd rather wait for him here, if that's all right with you.'

'Well, he could be several hours,' the constable replied dubiously. 'But you can wait if you want.'

He indicated a pair of slatted benches placed on the far side of the foyer and Stanley Aspinell retreated to one of them, the dog following him.

During the afternoon, the telephone rang several times and people came and went. In between dealing with the callers, the constable remembered the old man's presence and glanced across to where he was sitting. For the most part, he sat looking straight ahead in an attitude of patient resignation which people used to waiting learn to adopt. The dog seemed accustomed to it, too. After turning itself round awkwardly several times on the polished floor, it finally went to sleep in a rough pile of old fur, its nose tucked against its flank. From time to time, when the door opened or the telephone rang, it opened one eye momentarily. The next instant, the eye had snapped shut and the side of its face assumed the same blank appearance.

Despite his apparent resignation, Stanley Aspinell was more aware of his surroundings than the constable gave him credit for. Although he hardly changed his position on the hard bench, he absorbed the details of the place: the noticeboard with its posters of a man wanted by the Hertfordshire police on a rape charge, the anti-rabies precautions.

Further off, behind the door which led into the main building, he was conscious also of a hidden life going on that seemed to contain an air of controlled excitement and activity. The sounds of footsteps and voices filtered through, the almost constant ringing of telephones and the subdued clatter of typewriters in unseen rooms. Occasionally the action spilled out into the entrance hall where he waited. People came through the door, spoke briefly to the constable on duty and departed into the ordinary outside world; not always men in uniform but civilians, too. Seeing them, Stanley Aspinell wondered if they were clerks or plain-clothes detectives and he studied their appearance carefully as they went past, knowing that he might shortly be dealing with someone like them. He was reassured by the serious-faced, middle-aged men, downcast by a young man with long hair and dirty jeans who signed a piece of paper at the desk before sauntering out.

Was he a detective or a suspect allowed to leave because there was insufficient evidence?

71

Stanley Aspinell wondered and watched his departure uneasily.

He also watched the constable without appearing to do so, veiling his own eyes whenever the constable looked in his direction. The entrance hall and the desk constituted his little kingdom and he moved about it with a portly dignity despite his youth, taking his time before answering the telephone, sorting papers, writing things down with a ponderous seriousness which Stanley Aspinell had grudgingly to admire.

He, too, had served behind a counter all his life, in a seed merchant's in the town centre, now a ladies' shoe-shop, but he had never managed to achieve that unflustered, let-them-wait attitude. He remembered only the panic when the shop was crowded, the fumbling for change in the till drawer; the anxiety as he handed it over that he had made a mistake in adding up 4s. 11½d. and 5s.9d., aware of the manager's eye on him and that if he lost this job it wouldn't be easy to get another.

And all the time he was conscious of the round-faced clock on the wall and the progress of its hands towards four and then ten past, quarter past, twenty past.

At twenty-five past, catching the constable's glance directed towards him, Stanley Aspinell cast about in his mind for something to do which would make his presence less obvious, and, remembering the book on chess which was still in his pocket, he got it out and, turning the pages, pretended to be absorbed in its contents.

Inside Holly Lodge, Finch also checked the time. It was half past four. The body had been removed, carried down the steep steps in a body bag under the curious eyes of the bystanders, although now that the light was fading and the late afternoon was growing cold only the most persistent remained. The door-to-door inquiries at the immediate houses had been completed and some of the men, having given Finch a short verbal report, had already left.

It was time for them all to go apart from a uniformed officer who would remain on duty at the gate to dissuade the over curious from tramping about the garden or attempting to enter the house.

At the top of the steps, Finch paused to look back at the building. It was a strange place for murder, he thought, although on second thoughts perhaps it made an ideal setting. Framed in the holly arch, with its lights out and the grey brick façade in darkness, it had a brooding, secretive air.

'Aren't you coming, sir?' Boyce demanded.

He was standing at the door of the car, trying to conceal his impatience, aching for hot tea and a chance to sit down.

Finch descended the steps, acknowledging the salute of the man on duty before getting in beside Boyce. As they drew away from the kerb and the last bystanders began to disperse reluctantly, the other remaining cars also moved off.

They entered the brightly-lit foyer at divisional headquarters in a group, Finch leading the way, Boyce, Munro and some of the others following immediately behind them.

At the desk, Finch stopped to address the two Sergeants.

'In my office in ten minutes,' he told them. 'I want to make a short briefing on the case so far. Meanwhile, get yourselves tea and something to eat in the canteen. The rest of you can push off although I'd like your reports first thing in the morning.'

As the men moved away, Boyce first off the mark, Finch noticed with amusement, the desk constable caught his attention.

'There's someone here to see you, sir. He's been waiting nearly all afternoon; says he's got some information on the Temperance Street case.'

The constable suddenly stiffened in the act of nodding his head to indicate the benches. Turning, Finch saw they were empty.

'What man?' he asked.

Emerging from behind the counter, the constable came forward as if to verify the fact for himself and stared at the empty seats.

'Well, he was here a few minutes ago.' He sounded defensive as if the Chief Inspector doubted the man's existence. 'I saw him myself. He was an elderly bloke with a dog. He must have slipped out as you came in.'

'Name and address?' Finch demanded.

The constable retreated behind the desk, putting it between himself and the Chief Inspector.

'He wouldn't leave them, sir. He said he wanted to talk to you personally. He wouldn't even let on what the information was except it was to do with the murder at Holly Lodge; said he'd been outside there this afternoon but it didn't seem he liked to bother you while you were on the case. I tried to get him to say who he was, but it was no good.'

'Oh, hell,' Finch said softly, at which the constable pressed his chin down against his collar. 'What did he look like?'

'Elderly, like I said, sir. Short; grey hair. Rather nervous. Kept looking at the clock. The dog was a brown and white mongrel, a bit scruffy-looking. He had a book he was reading.'

'Is this it?' Finch asked, stooping down to retrieve a grey-covered book which had slipped down on to the floor behind one of the benches. It had a picture of a black knight and the words *Chess for Enthusiasts* printed on the cover.

'It looks like it, sir,' the constable replied, brightening up as if the book proved without any doubt the man's existence.

There was something else printed on the cover, Finch noticed, a name and address: E. Beach, Secondhand Dealer, 54 Thackeray Street.

Holding the book in his hand, Finch went in search of Boyce whom he found in the canteen with a cup of tea and a half-eaten cheese sandwich in front of him.

'I've got a job for you,' Finch told him.

Boyce stopped chewing and looked wary.

'What sort of job?'

'I want you to go round to this address and make inquiries. We're looking for an elderly man with a dog who must have bought this book off Beach. According to the desk constable, he was waiting to pass on some information on the Temperance Street inquiry but he cleared off as soon as we arrived.'

'Funny,' Boyce remarked.

'That's what I thought. Anyway, try and trace him if you can and find out what he knows. Take a DPC with you.' Glancing round the crowded tables, he added, 'Bannister will do.'

'What about the briefing?' Boyce asked, shoving the last piece of cheese sandwich into his mouth and swilling it down with a swig of tea.

'I'll go over the case with Munro meanwhile,' Finch replied. Seeing Boyce's expression take on a closed, hostile look, he added, 'If you're not back in time, I'll fill you in later myself, Tom, over a pint.'

It was a sop. All the same, Boyce didn't seem all that mollified. Getting to his feet and putting the book into his pocket, he merely nodded before going off to collect Bannister.

Munro, too, seemed subdued when later he joined Finch in his office.

'Boyce not here?' he asked.

'He's gone off on an inquiry,' Finch replied. In some ways, he thought guiltily, it was better without Tom. He and Colin Munro could go over the background of the case more quickly in Boyce's absence and certainly he welcomed the loss of tension which was always generated between the two men, largely due to Boyce's influence. 'Right,' he continued, 'let's get some of the details of what we know out of the way first before we plan our next move. Firstly, the dead man had only been living in that house a few days. According to Jenner who was on the door-to-door inquiries, the woman living opposite noticed lights on for the first time on Wednesday evening.'

'Did she see anyone?' Munro asked.

'I was coming to that,' Finch said a little snappishly. He had noticed before a tendency on Munro's part to jump the gun with questions. It showed keenness, he supposed, but nevertheless it was an exasperating habit. 'She saw a young, fair-haired man leave the house on a couple of occasions, presumably the man we found murdered, but she saw no one else although she noticed a car parked outside yesterday evening at about half past seven. But no,' he continued quickly, before Munro could speak, 'she couldn't even give a good description of it except it was black. No one else seems to have noticed a bloody thing. By the way, Kyle reported back. He's traced the name and address of the landlord of the house. He's called Fuller and he lives in Bermondsey. I'm sending Kyle and Gordon off tomorrow to interview the man and find out if he can tell us a bit more about his tenant and in whose name the place was rented.'

He spoke more rapidly than he was accustomed to, forced to run on in order to keep Munro and his damned questions at bay.

'What about you?' he added. 'What have you turned up?'

'Not a lot, sir,' Munro admitted. 'The landlord of the Carpenters' Arms thought he recognized the man by the description. Someone like him has been in there a couple of lunchtimes and evenings during the latter part of this week. Not last night, though – Friday.'

'So it's possible he was drinking at some other pub,' Finch suggested. He was thinking of the car seen parked outside the house. Had someone called to take the man out for a drink, possibly his murderer?

'Could be, sir,' Munro agreed. 'I could check the pubs in the area. I'll also go back to the Carpenters' Arms later with a photograph of the dead man to make sure of the ID. It was the same at the fish-and-chip shop and the Chinese take-away on the corner of Argylle Street. A man answering the same description has been seen in both places over the last couple of days. He was always alone, by the way.'

'It doesn't give us a lot to go on,' Finch said gloomily. 'There's the furniture, of course. It looks new so the chances are it was bought recently. It's too late to make a start on it now, but first thing on Monday morning I'd like you and Boyce to go round the local shops making inquiries – not just the furniture shops but any place that might deal in that sort of stuff.'

'Stores selling camping equipment?' Munro suggested brightly.

'That's what I had in mind,' Finch replied with a heavy air.

'By the way,' Munro added, 'about the furniture, sir. As it was being packed up for forensic, I noticed there were some small numbered labels stuck on the underside of the frames. I thought they might be the manufacturer's or wholesaler's numbering. If it is, it could help us in tracing them.'

'That's a bit of good luck,' Finch remarked, brightening up.

It was time something positive happened, if it were only a few labels. 'Anything else?'

'That's the lot, sir.'

'Then let's run over quickly what we know. Firstly, the man moved into the house on Wednesday. Secondly, a car was seen parked outside at about half past seven yesterday evening. Then this morning someone made an anonymous telephone call reporting his murder, possibly his murderer although I doubt it. If I'd just bashed someone's head in, I'd clear off and say nothing, especially as the chances were it'd be days before the body was discovered. Nothing's known about the caller, not even where the call was made from although it was a pay-box. He had a Cockney voice according to the Sergeant who took the call, but that's nothing to go on these days. We've no ID on the victim either. I suppose someone will report him missing eventually, although we can't even be sure of that.'

As he made each point, it occurred to Finch how many of them were negative. No ID, no witnesses, not even the time of death established with any accuracy, although Marion Greave would no doubt do her best. As her image rose in his mind, he deliberately pushed it away. It was not the time to start thinking of her. He must keep his head clear for the investigation.

Infuriatingly, Munro voiced his thoughts.

'It's not much to go on, sir.'

Finch was spared having to reply. Boyce chose the moment to knock and enter the office, stiffening up as he saw Munro already installed.

'Sit down, Tom,' Finch said in his friendliest voice. 'Did you find him?'

'No, sir,' Boyce replied, deliberately placing his own chair a little distance from Munro's, 'although I found out his name and address. I got them from the chap Beach. He owns a secondhand shop and it seems he gave the book to a friend of his called Stanley Aspinell. They play chess together every Friday evening.'

'Friday?' Finch broke in eagerly. 'Did they meet last night for a game?'

'Yes, they did as a matter of fact. Aspinell mentioned to

Beach that he'd seen lights on in Holly Lodge on his way to Beach's house. So I went round to Aspinell's house to check. He only lives a short distance away from Temperance Street, in Charlton Road, number seventeen.'

'What did he say?'

'He wasn't in,' Boyce replied with gloomy satisfaction, 'although the old biddy next door came nipping out the minute I knocked; must have been watching from behind the front room curtains. She told me Aspinell was out, probably baby-sitting for his daughter. He quite often goes over to her house on a Saturday evening. He's a widower and lives alone.'

'Her name and address?' Finch asked.

'That's the trouble,' Boyce replied. 'The old girl didn't know. All she knew was the daughter is called Marilyn and the son-in-law's Martin. She thinks he works in a garage some-where which wasn't a lot of help either.'

'You'll have to call back there later tonight,' Finch remarked.

Boyce's gloomy satisfaction deepened.

'I think it'll be a waste of time. It seems Aspinell often spends the night at his daughter's. The son-in-law drives him back Sunday morning.'

'In that case, we'll both go over to interview him tomorrow morning,' Finch said. He was about to add a brief apologetic remark about spoiling Boyce's Sunday morning, knowing the Sergeant had planned to take his wife to her sister's for the day, when a clerk, after knocking and entering the room, handed the Chief Inspector a printed sheet.

'This has just come through on the teleprinter, sir,' he said. 'I thought you'd like to have it straight away.'

Finch read it quickly.

'Wanted for questioning in connection with the murder of PC Flower of E Division, Hampstead, on the evening of Thursday October 21st and also for burglary,' it ran, 'Frank Charles Garston, aged 34, 6'2", broad-build, dark brown hair; club owner; from the Bermondsey district of London. Also Raymond John Chivers, aged 24, 5'11", medium build, fair wavy hair; electrician; also from the Bermondsey area. Anyone with information regarding these men and their present whereabouts should communicate immediately with Detective Chief Superintendent Nunn of New Scotland Yard.'

It was the second description which caught Finch's attention. Glancing across at the two Sergeants as he reached for the telephone and began dialling, he said briefly, 'I think we've got an ID on our murder victim. He's wanted on a murder charge of his own.'

He did not add, as he might have done, that the name of the Detective Chief Superintendent at the end of the print-out was familiar to him.

It would be a great pleasure, Finch thought as the call was connected, to work with Reggie Nunn on a case once again.

6

After he returned to the cottage, Hugo spent the afternoon working in the garden. It was protected from the surrounding fields by high hawthorn hedges which the wind could not penetrate so that he had the illusion of being inside an oblong box composed of leaves, grass and earth, open only to the sky, an elemental shelter which he found comforting.

The work satisfied him, too. It demanded nothing from him except mindless labour: cutting, hacking, burning. He had not stayed at the cottage since the visit there with Ray at the end of the summer and, in the intervening weeks, the nettles had sprung up again and the brambles had regrown. Slashing them back, he felt appeased. The destruction left behind a rough order which seemed symbolic. It was a crude beginning on which he might rebuild although he did not allow himself to think too far ahead.

In one corner of the garden, a young birch sapling had established itself, the seed from which it had grown dropped there perhaps by a bird or blown in by the wind. When he had first found it under a smother of nettles, he had been curiously moved by its stubborn, tenacious hold on life and had allowed it to remain, cutting back the surrounding weeds to let the air and sunlight penetrate. Over the years, he had watched it grow from that fragile beginning until now it stood several feet high and its slender trunk with the pale, papery bark shone out like a wand against the closer, denser thickets of the hawthorns. In spring, it put out shrill green leaves which in summer were light-veined against the sun. Even now, in autumn, stripped of its foliage, it still retained its delicate beauty, the fine twigs showering down like strands of hair. He thought of it absurdly as *his* tree, as if he had personally planted and nourished it and the miracle of its growth was entirely his responsibility.

Stooping down to clear the grass from round its roots and to strip back the thin tendrils of ivy which, creeping insidiously upwards, threatened to engulf its trunk, he rested one hand for a moment against its bark and felt it as smooth and cool as flesh beneath his palm. In the greyish gloom of the late afternoon, it possessed a luminosity as if the whole tree had been drenched in moonlight.

To his right, as he worked through the gathering dusk, the cottage settled down into the landscape, absorbed into the surrounding trees and bushes until it lost its detail and it became a mere outline against the darkening sky, the steep cat's-slide of the back elevation of the roof, with its one casement window set like a Cyclop's eye in the thatch, merging with the timbers and old brick of the walls. Only the chimney remained a visible entity, perched up above the long, low line of the ridge to signify that it was a habitation and not a haystack or a denser mass of leaves.

At five o'clock, when the last light dwindled, he went inside the cottage carrying an armful of small, broken branches and, without bothering to put on the lamps, kindled a fire in the sitting-room hearth. The twigs caught quickly, small bright flames shooting up into the blackened chimney opening as the thin wood crackled and exploded. When it was well alight, Hugo laid larger logs across the grate and watched the flames bend round them, feeling their way between the crevices while yellowish smoke poured from the cracks in the bark.

There was always a moment when the fire seemed to hold

itself in balance and the whole edifice might collapse into a ruin of smouldering, half-burnt wood. Tonight, as he watched, one flame steadied itself above the logs and then leapt upwards. Another joined it and fine white ash, still sparkling, dropped below the bars.

Straightening up, Hugo felt absurdly triumphant. Now that the fire was burning, other tasks could be completed and, switching on the lamps and drawing the curtains, he prepared for the evening which lay ahead with an anticipation that almost amounted to pleasure. Even Ray's absence seemed distanced and there were whole moments when, cooking a meal for himself, Hugo forgot his existence.

He ate by the fireside, a tray across his lap, the radio playing Vivaldi softly in the background. Sitting there, it was possible to re-imagine, however briefly, what had drawn him to this place originally, long before Ray's arrival: the sense of privacy which it created and a simplicity which demanded nothing from him.

It was satisfyingly basic, composed of four rooms, two down and two up, with a tiny bathroom fitted in over a small square hall from which the staircase led upwards between walls of bulging plaster. In response to its uncomplicated structure and perhaps to satisfy some ascetic need in himself, he had made no attempt to convert it into the conventional weekend cottage, retaining the uneven walls and the worn brick floors. Its furniture was plain, almost monkish. Everything had been chosen because it was functional, not decorative. It was mostly stuff he had picked up cheaply at country auctions and which suited the bare, low-ceilinged rooms and the atmosphere which he had liked to think was linked to the fundamental truths of birth, work and death, an attitude which he now realized was mere self-deceptive, romantic escapism. At fifty, he was too old for such a simplistic, child-like retreat from reality. But it had taken Ray to make him realize that life was not really like that. It was made up of much smaller considerations: trivial deceits and petty pleasures, emotions which passed as rapidly and as fleetingly as cloud shadows across grass.

To endure was all that mattered.

As he carried the tray into the kitchen, the headlamps of a car swept across the uncurtained window and then halted, pointing up the lane.

Someone got out. He heard the door slam and then the car drew away, its lights dipping and swooping across the trees, illuminating them momentarily.

Footsteps approached the cottage along the shingled drive.

Hugo was at the front door even before the caller knocked.

It must be Ray! There was no one else it could be. He must have hired a taxi and driven over from Chelmsford in order to bring about a reconciliation. The impulsive, spur-of-the-moment decision was typical of him. There would be laughter, Hugo thought happily, and for once he would know exactly what to say.

As he opened the door, he could envisage Ray standing there, wearing that ridiculous pale blue, shiny parka, his hands stuffed deep into his pockets and that little, lop-sided smile on his face which always indicated embarrassment. Hugo had even extended an arm to place across Ray's shoulders to draw him into the hall.

The sight of the stranger on the doorstep shocked and bewildered him. For a moment, he registered but did not recognize the sharp, tightly-bunched features and the smooth-fitting black hair growing close to the scalp, although the man seemed to know him. Peering in at the brightly-lit hall, he asked, 'I've got the right address, haven't I? You are Hugo?'

'Yes, I am,' Hugo replied stiffly. There was an air of jaunty familiarity about the man which he resented. Then, as he spoke, recognition dawned. Remembering the figure he had glimpsed standing in the porch of Holly Lodge, he added in surprise, 'You're Ray's brother, Benny.'

'Yeah, that's right,' Benny replied laconically. 'Aren't you going to ask me in?'

'You'd better come through to the sitting-room,' Hugo said. He was uncertain how to react, feeling that the man's presence was an intrusion and yet, as Ray's brother, some welcome had to be extended to him. He noticed for the first time that Benny was carrying a suitcase which he dumped down just inside the sitting-room before crossing to the fire where he held his hands out to the flames. He gave the impression of making himself at home which Hugo found offensive.

As if in explanation and apology, although there was nothing contrite about his voice, Benny said over his shoulder, 'Nice to see a fire. It's a bit parky out there this evening. You wouldn't happen to have a drop of whisky about the place, would you?'

His bright black eyes had already established the presence of the decanter and glasses on the serving table.

As he poured the drink, Hugo was able to consider for the first time the implications behind Benny's arrival.

Ray must have given him the address. There was no other way Benny could have acquired it. And that suggested that Ray and Benny must have discussed him between themselves, a realization which angered Hugo. Ray had no right to pass on any information, not even to his brother, unless of course Ray was in some kind of trouble . . .

'Is Ray all right?' he asked, turning with quick anxiety to hand the glass to Benny.

Benny drank before replying, seating himself in Hugo's chair by the fire. Putting down the glass, he loosened his overcoat, deliberately taking his time. Even then he didn't answer directly.

'Yeah, I had a hell of a job getting here,' he said as if in reply to an entirely different question. 'I went up to London first from Chelmsford; then changed my mind and caught another train from Liverpool St down to Manningtree. A bit off the beaten track, aren't you? The taxi driver hadn't heard of the place. He had to ask the way at the pub.' He paused before adding, 'Ray? He's all right, I suppose.'

'Then why are you here?' Hugo asked, making no effort to disguise his impatience.

'I need somewhere to stay for a while, somewhere quiet. Ray mentioned this place and it sounded just what I was looking for. No neighbours, no one snooping about asking questions. Ray said it was at the back of beyond . . .'

'You can't stay,' Hugo interrupted him. 'I'm only down here myself for the weekend. I'm going back to London tomorrow.

And I might add that I think you've got a bloody nerve, simply turning up and expecting hospitality even if you are Ray's brother.'

'Mates,' Benny said and, seeing the expression on Hugo's face, added in further explanation, 'Me and Ray aren't brothers. He's a mate of mine, that's all; boyfriend if you want to know the truth. We have been for years although we weren't exclusive. It wasn't that kind of a set-up. We both felt free to have other affairs.' He was clearly enjoying the situation, watching Hugo's reactions with bright-eyed malevolence over the rim of his glass. 'Does that surprise you? Did you think Ray was faithful, the little blue-eyed boy all fresh and innocent?'

Hugo ran his tongue over his lips before replying.

'I want you to leave immediately otherwise I shall call the police.'

'I shouldn't do that if I was you,' Benny replied. He had settled himself back comfortably into the chair and his voice, no longer derisive, had taken on a reasonable, almost conversational, tone. 'Because we're in the shit up to our necks, Hugo, old buddy, thanks to Ray. You and me both. I don't know what yarn Ray told you, but, knowing him, I bet it sounded good and you believed him. It was always hard to tell when Ray was lying, even for me and I've known him for years. So let's start off with a few facts, shall we? Number one: Ray was on the run after he and a couple of mates robbed a house in Hampstead and a copper got killed. You probably heard about it on the news. I was down in Brighton at the time, otherwise he'd've come to me for help, the stupid berk, not you. That's how you got drawn in. Fact number two: Ray's dead. I found him this morning at the house. Somebody's bashed his head in and it don't take much imagination to work out why he did it. Ray must have had a few thousand quid on him, the proceeds from that burglary, and whoever killed him helped himself to it. So it has to be someone in the know, one of his so-called mates down in Bermondsey. Ray must have blabbed to someone; he never knew when to keep his frigging mouth shut, although how in the hell they traced him down to Chelmsford, Christ alone knows. I haven't worked that bit out yet. Only me and you knew the address and

I certainly didn't talk.' He cocked a speculative eye at Hugo and then grinned derisively. 'And I don't seriously reckon it was you either. You're not likely to be mixed up with Ray's East End friends, are you? It could be Garston, of course. He was with Ray on the Hampstead job and he's still on the run. It's his style, too – a quick bash over the head. That's how Ray bought it. Anyhow, I wasn't hanging about to find out, either at the house or back in London; I know too much already. If Garston or one of his side-kicks isn't out looking for me, then the police are. Even the most bone-headed copper is going to connect me sooner or later with Ray and I don't fancy being picked up by either mob, ta very much. That's why I've come here. There's nowhere else I could go.'

While Benny was speaking, Hugo had backed away slowly step by step to the far side of the fireplace where he stood looking down at Benny sprawled negligently in the armchair, his legs stretched out in front of the fire and the half-empty glass of whisky held in both hands against his chest. As if from a great distance, Hugo heard the casual, slightly nasal voice running on and on as he watched the peaks and hollows of the man's face lifting and falling with the movements of speech. Only the hair remained static: that black, shining cap which appeared to have so little connection with the rest of his features.

He had no doubt that Benny was speaking the truth. Despite the feeling of being only distantly involved so that any emotional response seemed to be drowned before it could reach him, he was sufficiently aware of the reality of the situation for his judgement to remain unimpaired.

It all made sense: a terrifying, appalling sense. Ray's lies and deceits which Hugo had half-suspected could no longer be held in question and he saw now what a fool he had been to allow himself to be even partly persuaded by them.

All the same, when he finally spoke, his voice seemed to come echoing back from across the same void from which he listened to Benny and he heard himself repeating stupidly, 'Ray's dead?'

Benny sat up straight and drained his glass.

'Yeah, that's right.'

His voice was curt, like a slap round the face and Hugo shuddered as if in contact with an actual, physical blow. The sudden reaction seemed to shake him into an awareness of what was happening.

'And it was murder?' he demanded.

Benny was watching him warily, conscious of a new alertness in Hugo and unsure in what form it might express itself.

'He didn't bash his own head in,' he replied.

'Do the police know?'

'I made a 999 call on the way to the station but I didn't leave a name.'

'They must be told everything,' Hugo said, coming to a decision. He even turned towards the door.

Behind him, he heard Benny's voice raised in shrill, alarmed derision.

'What about, for God's sake? About the Hampstead job? They know all that already. And about the copper Garston killed. So what the hell are you going to tell them? That Ray was your lover? That you were helping him while he was on the run? Because that's what they'll think. Or are you hoping your upper-class accent will see you right? Let me tell you something, old buddy, the prisons are full of blokes like you – public school con-men and bent accountants with university degrees . . .'

Hugo didn't wait to hear the rest of it. Slamming the front door behind him, he stumbled across the lawn to where the car was parked in the driveway, thanking God the keys to it were in his trouser pocket.

The night had closed in and it was darker than he had anticipated. There was no moon and even the stars were muffled behind low, drifting clouds. In contrast, the car head-lamps lit up too brilliantly the surrounding trees and bushes, bringing each twig and leaf rushing forward into sudden, dazzling proximity.

The nearest telephone box was half a mile away in the village, or rather the small group of cottages and houses which, together with the public house, the Wheatsheaf, and a general shop, constituted the hamlet of Lambourne. The kiosk was placed on an empty stretch of verge opposite the shop which was closed, its blind drawn.

Leaving the side lights on, Hugo pulled open the door, feeling broken glass crunch under his feet, probably from the bulb because there was no light in there. A faint illumination came from the houses across the road but not enough to read the directory to find the number of the nearest police station.

He could call the operator, of course, or ring 999 as Benny had done; perhaps the latter course would be best because, when the operator gave him the number of a police station it would not be easy dialling it in the dark. Lifting the receiver, he felt for the slots in the dial, trying to think of nothing except carrying out this simple action, not Ray's death nor Benny's parting words. As for his own future, that was an enormity which he did not even dare to consider.

Benny rose to his feet as Hugo re-entered the sitting-room, searching his face with a bright, alert gaze. He was still wearing his unbuttoned overcoat as if in readiness for departure but, after one look at Hugo's expression as he crossed the room to pour himself a whisky, Benny gave a small, hardly audible laugh of triumph and, taking off his coat, threw it down over the back of the chair.

'You didn't phone them,' he said. It was a statement, not a question.

When Hugo didn't reply, Benny came to stand beside him, holding out his own empty glass which Hugo filled for him.

'You did the right thing, Hugo, old friend,' Benny continued, his voice soft and intimate. 'There's no point in stirring up the shit more than you have to. Ray's dead. What good would it do him if you drop us further in it? You've got your career of think, haven't you? It could muck up your reputation if it got known you were mixed up in something like this. Me, I've got less to lose but I still enjoy my freedom.'

'How long do you want to stay?' Hugo asked abruptly, not looking at him.

Benny took his glass back to the fire.

'A couple of weeks. Maybe a month. Just long enough to get things sorted. I've got some papers I had fixed up for Ray. As he won't be needing them now, I might as well make use of them. But I'd like things to quieten down a bit first before I push off. It'll also give me time to suss out just how much the police know by listening to the news on the radio. As I don't reckon they've found out about this place yet, it'll suit me down to the ground.' Feet planted slightly apart, he stood in front of the fire, looking about him with an easy, proprietorial air. 'Yeah, I like it here. As a matter of fact while you were out phoning, or rather not phoning, the police, I took the liberty of looking the place over. All mod cons, I noticed: bathroom, shower, even a deep-freeze in the kitchen well stocked up. Not much in the way of booze, though. Perhaps you wouldn't mind getting in a few bottles tomorrow before you push off back to London. I'd pay you only I'm a bit short of the ready.' He paused and as Hugo still remained silent, he picked up the monologue again in the same conversational manner. 'I can't understand why Ray didn't like it down here. Bored stiff, he was. But then Ray wasn't much good at amusing himself, was he? Liked the bright lights too much: a few laughs, a chance for a chat. That's probably why he got himself murdered. Too much of the gab. Me, I'm more of a loner. I like my own company. God knows why someone like you picked up with him in the first place. I shouldn't have thought he was your type.'

'I don't want to discuss him,' Hugo said coldly.

'Mind you, he was good-looking, I'll give him that,' Benny continued as if Hugo had not spoken. 'One of the pretty boys. And I don't suppose the relationship was all that serious, was it? I mean, someone in your position couldn't afford to be seen around with Ray. So it had to be a hole-in-the-corner affair: meeting in out-of-the-way pubs and hotels, no commitments and everything done on the sly. Not that I'm blaming you and I don't mind admitting that it was Ray's looks that first made me fall for him, but then I always was a sucker for blonds. And that skin! Even when he was a teenager, it was perfect. When the rest of us was worrying about acne, there was Ray looking like an advert for Max Factor.'

Despite himself, Hugo asked, 'Is that when you first met him?'

He had not intended to take part at all in the conversation, but felt himself drawn insidiously into it.

'Yeah, that's right. He was hanging about a boozer in Jamaica Road one evening. He'd just run away from home and didn't know what the hell to do, except he was looking for a good time. I was a few years older than him; knew my way round a bit. I'd got this flat so I took him in. Got him his first job, too, through someone I knew.'

'He told me it was his probation officer,' Hugo protested.

Benny laughed.

'Christ, that's Ray all over! He could never resist tarting up the facts. If you want to know the truth, the bloke who gave him the job was one of my ex-boyfriends, shit-scared that I'd phone his wife. So he did me a favour and took Ray on, in more senses than one if you get my meaning. Not that I really minded. As I said before, me and Ray weren't exclusive although he always came back to me in the end. Mind you, there *was* a probation officer. Ray was a bit light-fingered at times but until Garston got his mitts on him, he'd never got involved in any big-time crime. Garston did for him in more ways than one.'

His face sharpened as he spoke, the lips narrowing into a bitter line.

'How long had Ray known Garston?' Hugo asked and could tell by the way Benny looked at him with that bright, knowing glance that he had guessed the reason behind the question.

'About six months.' The thin mouth curved upwards. 'Not long after he'd met you, as a matter of fact. I said to him at the time, "What do you want to take up with rubbish like Garston for? Isn't one boyfriend at a time enough for you?" Because Garston was trash. You'd only got to look at him to see that. Nothing near your class, Hugo. All show – big car, flash clothes, diamond ring on his little finger; you know the type. Sorry, I'm forgetting, you probably don't. But Ray hadn't got a lot of taste where some men were concerned, you and me excepted, of course.'

So Ray was meeting Garston while he was having the affair

with me, Hugo thought. God, what a fool he must have thought me!

He recalled the evenings when Ray couldn't meet him, the weekends when he said he was working overtime, and the clear-eyed look Ray had given him as he made these excuses, his voice as he had said, 'But I'll see you tomorrow, Hugo. It'll be all the better for waiting.'

The memories were like ashes in Hugo's mouth and, as if the thoughts filled his mouth with actual dust, he pulled an expression of wry distaste as, turning away, he wiped his lips. It was the final betrayal.

Wasteland, he found himself thinking. A dead landscape with no hope of renewal. The stony land of the Bible on which no seed will grow.

'I'm going to have a bath,' he announced, addressing Benny without looking at him. 'If you want a meal, help yourself. You'll find everything you need in the kitchen. I shall leave early tomorrow morning. Oh, don't worry,' he added, as he saw Benny was about to interrupt him, 'I'll call at the pub before I go and make sure you're well stocked up. I take it whisky would suit you? And I'll be grateful if you could leave the cottage reasonably clean when you finally leave.'

His voice was clipped, the tone he always used to his junior staff or those who served him: distanced, polite, impersonal. He saw Benny step back and his features take on that ingratiating half-smile with which he was only too familiar. Even so, Benny tried a final throw.

'Which bedroom do you want me to sleep in, Hugo? Only I'm easy.'

The little fling of the shoulders, the tilt of his head were ridiculous, shaming. Hugo looked him up and down before replying.

'I'm not,' he said with cold dismissal. 'Use the back bedroom. You'll find sheets and blankets in there.'

Without a backward glance, he left the room.

The following morning, thank God, Benny had not got up by the time Hugo returned from the Wheatsheaf. Leaving the case of whisky in the kitchen together with the keys of the cottage for

Benny to find, he ignored the signs of his unwelcome presence: the egg-smeared plate and dirty cup in the sink, the overcoat still lying over the back of the armchair.

It didn't matter, he told himself as he drove away. He was finished with the place anyway. As soon as Benny had gone, he would put it on the market.

So much wasteland, he thought, although, as he turned into the lane, he found himself glancing into the rear mirror for a last glimpse of the birch tree, only to find that it was hidden from sight behind the house.

7

Detective Chief Superintendent Nunn stood with his hands behind his back, looking down without speaking at the face of the murdered man which the mortuary attendant had uncovered. For once he was silent, his brown, mobile features with the little, black boot-button eyes uncharacteristically still. Watching him from the other side of the trolley, Finch thought that he looked like a sad, wise monkey, contemplating with melancholy gravity yet another inexplicable example of human folly.

Finch had know Nunn for many years, since the time when they had both been Detective Sergeants and had worked together on a murder investigation which had involved the Yard. A friendship had developed between the two men, one of those easy-going relationships which had survived, despite the fact that Nunn's promotion had placed him in a higher rank than Finch's and they only met infrequently when a case, such as this one, brought them into contact with each other.

Still without speaking, Nunn nodded to the attendant who pulled the sheet over the face and began trundling the trolley backwards to the refrigerated drawer in which it had been stored. The faint clang of metal and the squeak of rubber tyres were magnified, as in a sounding box, by the tile and stainless steel of their surroundings. A tap dripped with persistent monotony into a sluice.

Outside in the corridor, beyond the swing door, Nunn spoke for the first time since he had entered the place, shaking himself as a dog might to rouse himself.

'That's Ray Chivers, all right,' he announced. 'And now, for God's sake let's get out of here, Jack. Even after all my years on the force, mortuaries still give me the willies. What I need now is a cold beer and a warm fire.'

Finch found him both in a small, back-street public house where there was still a snug, almost empty at that time on a Sunday morning apart from two old men playing dominoes at a corner table.

Carrying the two pint mugs back from the bar to the other corner where Nunn had established himself, Finch saw that he had cheered up and was looking about him with lively interest at the brown-painted lincrusta dado, the faded floral wallpaper above it and the coal fire, heaped up high in a little black iron grate with a vase of artificial daffodils on the mantelshelf.

'Nice here,' Nunn said appreciatively. 'Not many places like this left. They're all wall-to-wall carpeting these days and plastic wood.'

He spoke quickly in short sentences as if each word, as in a telegram, cost money and therefore had to be used sparingly, keeping his voice low in order not to be overheard.

'Raymond John Chivers,' he continued, picking up where he had left off outside the mortuary doors. 'Aged twenty-four. Electrician working for a firm of contractors in the King's Cross area. Not much form until now although when he was fourteen he was put on probation for street-stealing and not a lot known about his background. Brought up in Poplar. Mother died when he was eight. Father a docker, that is when he wasn't down the boozer. A younger brother and sister. The whole lot got taken into care after the mother died. Ray, as he was generally known, absconded from a children's home in Gravesend when he was fifteen and disappeared although we now know what happened to him. Come across Benny Costello yet?'

Finch shook his head. Knowing Nunn, it was better not to interrupt him when he was in full flight.

'A mate of Ray's in more senses than one. Grandfather was an Italian but Benny's as Cockney as they come. Six years older than Ray and a wide boy who always manages to keep one foot inside the law. Works the East End clubs mainly – barman, croupier, ponce, too, when necessary but prefers living off boyfriends if he gets the chance. Little, thin-faced bloke, as sharp as a razor blade. He and Ray shared a flat in Bermondsey. He probably initiated Ray into the gay scene. It's known Ray had boyfriends apart from Benny. Incidentally, it looks as if Benny's done a bunk. The flat's empty and he hasn't been seen there since Friday. We're trying to trace him but it's like looking for a rat in a sewer.'

'Do you think he could have killed Ray?' Finch asked, remembering that the man who had made the 999 call had spoken with a London accent.

Nunn shrugged.

'God knows. It's possible although it's not Benny's usual style. There's no history of violence. Benny's tactics are usually more subtle than that. A bit of blackmail, yes, but murder? Unlikely, not unless he had his back up against the wall. Now Garston . . . But's let's start at the beginning.

'Frank Garston – a real heavy. Done one stretch for GBH and a lot more's suspected – obtaining money with menaces, protection rackets, robbery – you name it, Garston's probably had a dabble in it at some time in his life. But legit. up front. Runs a club in Bermondsey which is probably where he got to know Ray and Benny. Bent as a corkscrew, if you get my meaning. Liked to have pretty boys round him which is why he picked up with Ray. But there were other motives as well. Garston doesn't do anything unless there's at least two good reasons.

'As I told you, Ray was an electrician and the firm he worked for often got commercial contracts – rewiring jobs at offices and warehouses, that sort of thing. A useful boy to have around from Garston's point of view. Ray could suss a place out, note where the alarms were and what sort of security system was in operation, make sketches of the layout. There have been a couple of break-ins at premises where Ray's firm had been working, but we didn't put two and two together until this last job.

'This was a private house in Hampstead owned by a man called Mitchell, a coin-dealer, or so he describes himself although I have my doubts as to how far he's honest but that's a problem for the Income Tax inspectors, not us, thank God. Anyhow, he owns a big, detached house standing in its own grounds. Mitchell lived there alone with what he called his butler – more like a bodyguard, if you ask me. No other live-in servants. About a month ago, Ray got sent there to put in new wall lights and other bits and pieces and while he was busy in the hall one afternoon, Mitchell came home and went into his study, leaving the door ajar. Now it just so happened that Ray had taken a mirror off the wall and it was propped up at such an angle that he could see into the study without Mitchell realizing it, so Ray was able to watch Mitchell cross the room, open the wall safe which was hidden behind a painting and shove a whole lot of money into it from his brief-case. There was more of the stuff inside the safe as well.

'Ray reported back to Garston that evening who hatched up a little plan. Ray got his orders and the next day he found out Mitchell's telephone number, which is ex-directory, and kept his eyes generally skinned. They also kept a watch on the house, at least, Kenny Webber did. He's one of Garston's side-kicks who does the hard, dirty work for him. Webber noticed that on Thursday evenings the butler or bodyguard had the evening off and Mitchell was alone in the house. I got all this information, by the way, from Webber himself. We picked him up late Friday afternoon but had to squeeze the story out of him. Talk about getting blood out of stone! That's why the description of Ray Chivers wasn't circulated until yesterday.

'Anyway, to get back to Garston. The plan he thought up was so damned simple it's almost laughable. After a few discreet enquiries, Garston found out the name of the Crime Prevention Officer at the local nick who'd be likely to deal with any problems at Mitchell's house such as a break-in. Mitchell knew him by name; in fact, he'd asked the officer's advice when he'd had his alarm system fitted. So, on Thursday evening, after the butler had left, Garston phoned Mitchell and spun him some yarn about ringing on behalf of Sergeant Fletcher. There'd been a report of some suspicious-looking characters seen hanging about at the back of Mitchell's house and would it be all right if he and a couple of his plain-clothes colleagues called round to check?

'And Mitchell fell for it. As far as he could see, there was nothing suspicious about it. The name Sergeant Fletcher and the fact that the man who called him knew his ex-directory number made it all sound convincing. Shortly afterwards, there was a ring at the front door. Mitchell did take the precaution of having a quick dekko through the spy-hole and what did he see? Two men in plain-clothes and a uniformed Sergeant: Garston, in fact, in a hired get-up. Garston flourished what looked like an ID card and Mitchell let them in.

'As far as our little gang of three's concerned, it was a push-over. Mitchell's an elderly bloke with no taste for violence and it didn't take them long to persuade him to open the safe. They were lucky. Mitchell had planned a deal for the next day, a cash transaction which is what makes me feel he may be fiddling the books, and there was forty thousand quid in the safe, as well as a whole lot of Krugerrands. Garston and his two helpers stripped it bare, tied Mitchell up, ripped out the phones and they were off. In all, it took them about ten minutes. Mitchell, by the way, wasn't discovered until hours later when his butler came home.

'And then, on their way back to the car, their luck ran out. It was a car Garston had hired under a false name and, being a flash bloke, he'd opted for a brand new BMW. It so happened that, just as they were getting in it, an off-duty policeman, PC Flower, passed them on his way home. A bright lad, Flower, he noticed the car and a uniformed copper getting into it with two civilians – not the usual transport you'd expect even CID to be buzzing about in. Besides, he didn't recognize any of the men as coming from his station. So, being a conscientious sort of bloke, he walked over to have a word with them.

'Garston smashed him in the face with the cosh he'd threatened Mitchell with, which he still had in his pocket.'

'Cosh?' Finch put in quickly.

'A bloody great spanner to be precise. And if that wasn't enough, Garston ran over Flower as they made off. The car was later found abandoned on the Embankment. That's where they split up. According to Webber, Garston divided up the loot between them: fifteen thousand in cash to Webber, and twenty-five thousand to Ray Chivers because he'd put them on to the job in the first place. Garston kept the major part of the haul, the Krugerrands: something like fifty thousand quids' worth but, as Webber explained, Garston knew of a fence who'd handle them for him. Ray Chivers and Webber didn't have that kind of contact. Besides, neither of them was going to argue the toss with Garston.

'The three of them then cleared off, Garston, God knows where. We're still looking for him. As I said, we picked up Webber on Friday afternoon. He was bunking in with a girlfriend of his, a prostitute, in Blackfriars, but as soon as she found out about the dead copper, she turned him in. Besides, he was ruining her trade, hanging about her flat all day long. As for Ray Chivers . . .'

He left the sentence unfinished, cocking an inquiring eye at Finch who took up the account.

'We found him on Saturday morning, following an anony-mous 999 call at 11.27 am. At the time, of course, we didn't know who he was. It wasn't until later that afternoon when I got back to headquarters and saw the description of Ray Chivers that I realized he could be the man you were looking for.'

'Any leads?' Nunn asked eagerly.

'Not a lot so far,' Finch confessed, 'although there's a few possibilities we're following up. He'd evidently moved into the house where we found him last Wednesday . . .'

'Wednesday?' Nunn interrupted him. 'But that means he must have been holed up somewhere else for nearly a week.'

'Exactly, but I've no idea where. The house he was living in had been empty for several weeks. It was due for demolition and it was obvious he was only camping out there temporarily. The furniture was new: folding chairs and table and a camp bed. I'm trying to get them traced. If we can find out where they were bought, it might give us some useful leads. As I told you on the phone, he'd been struck on the side of the head by some blunt weapon . . .'

'Sounds like Garston,' Nunn commented. 'We'll know better once we've picked him up. Any dabs?'

'We're still checking on them. Someone had gone over the place wiping some of the surfaces but not all. We found at least two sets of prints, Ray Chivers' and someone else's which we haven't identified yet. I'll pass them on to you so that you can check them against Garston's record.'

'What about the money from the robbery? Chivers should have had that twenty-five thousand on him.'

'Nothing,' Finch replied, 'although it looks as if something had been hidden behind a gas fire in one of the bedrooms. It could have been a small suitcase or a box, judging by the marks left behind in the dust.'

'So whoever murdered him probably robbed him as well?' Nunn said thoughtfully.

'It's possible and it could provide a motive.'

'Unless the killer wanted Ray's mouth shut because he knew too much. On either count, Garston would fit the bill. He's a greedy man and he's also a frightened one.'

'But now that you've got Webber in custody, what good would it do Garston to get rid of Ray Chivers? I assume Webber will testify against Garston.'

'Not necessarily,' Nunn replied. 'It's a long way between arresting someone and getting him into a witness box. Garston's got contacts even inside Brixton prison. It wouldn't take much to persuade Webber to withdraw his statement and refuse to give evidence against Garston in court either by offering him a large sum of money once he's served his bird or threatening him with a bit of rough stuff while he's inside. It's been known to happen. Webber's only got to plead he was verballed by the police officers who took down his statement and the case against Garston goes out of the window. Mitchell can't identify any of them. Apart from that one glimpse through the peep-hole, he didn't see their faces. By the time he got the door open, they'd pulled stocking-masks on over their heads and they were careful to wear gloves so they didn't leave any dabs. With Flower dead, there'd only be Webber and Chivers for Garston to worry about and he may have reckoned that, once Ray was out of the way, it wouldn't take much to nobble Webber.'

'Could be,' Finch agreed. 'And I may be able to help you there. We've got a possible witness, name of Aspinell. I haven't had a chance to interview him yet; he was away from home last night but I'm calling to see him this afternoon. It seemed he turned up at headquarters early yesterday, soon after Chivers' murder was discovered, and told the desk constable he'd got information which he refused to pass on to anyone except me. I was still at the scene of the crime. Funny thing,' he added, 'after waiting for several hours, he cleared off without saying anything just as I got back. That's why I haven't been able to interview him yet.'

'Got cold feet?' Nunn suggested.

'God knows. He's an elderly man, according to the constable, and a bit on the nervous side. It's possible the sight of all of us turning up frightened him off. I'll have a quiet word with him later. It occurred to me he might have seen someone entering the house. According to a friend of his, a man called Beach, Aspinell knew the house, Holly Lodge, where the murder was committed and commented on the fact that he'd seen a light on in there.'

Nunn's face brightened.

'So if he did see someone and it was Garston, this man Aspinell might be able to pick him out at an ID parade once we've pulled him in. Christ, that'd really make my day! Any murder's bad enough but the cold-blooded killing of a copper, especially a young bloke with a wife and kids, makes me wish they'd never abolished hanging. I know I shouldn't say this and it's strictly off the record, but when you're dealing with someone like Garston . . . ' He broke off and continued more quietly, glancing sideways at the two elderly men on the other side of the snug, 'Honestly, though, Jack, it gets right up my nose sometimes. What the hell do the general public want? One minute they're screaming bloody blue murder about law and order, the next they're complaining because their rates have gone up to pay for the police force. And when a few bent coppers get rumbled, it's splashed across the headlines of every newspaper. Mind you, I'm all for rooting out the rotten apples, but when someone like Garston thinks he can manipulate the system and get away with it, you begin to wonder who we're protecting, the ordinary law-abiding citizen or the bloody criminals!'

Finch merely nodded, wary of being drawn into any discussion with Nunn whose opinions he knew could be emotional when roused. He also suspected that, once Nunn had calmed down, he would probably regret having expressed himself so forcibly to someone who, although a friend of many years' standing, was also junior to him in rank.

'There's another piece of information you might find useful,' he said, adroitly changing the subject, 'that's the name of the landlord who owned the house where Ray Chivers' body was found.' Taking out his notebook, he dictated it out loud while Nunn wrote it down. 'Charles Henry Fuller, 16 Grayson Road, Bermondsey.'

'An East End address,' Nunn commented almost to himself.

'One of my detective constables has gone up to London this morning to interview him so I can't tell you much about him except he seems to own several properties in this area, mostly the older type terraced houses which are scheduled for demolition. We've got nothing against him on our records but rumour has it that he wasn't the ideal landlord. He took the rent but that's about as far as it went. He made little effort to keep the properties in good repair or to modernize them. As they're all freehold, my guess is he was interested more in the land they stood on, especially as some of them are in prime redevelopment areas. When Kyle gets back, I'll let you know what he's found out about Fuller.'

'Thanks, Jack,' Nunn said, putting his notebook away in his inside pocket and buttoning up his overcoat. 'Is that the lot?'

'For the moment.'

'Give me a bell if anything else turns up.'

'Will do,' Finch agreed.

'And now I'd better be shoving off. I know you're busy and I want to get back to the hunt for Garston. I'll be a happy man when he's safely banged up.'

His face crinkled up with pleasure at the prospect.

After Nunn had left, Finch returned to his office where he found Boyce mooning about, looking gloomily out of the window.

'Kyle's not back yet,' he announced with an air of sombre satisfaction the moment Finch stepped inside the room. 'Any luck at the mortuary?'

He didn't appear all that cheered when Finch told him that Nunn had identified the dead man as Ray Chivers.

'Oh, God,' he said when Finch had finished his brief summary of Nunn's information, 'so this case looks as if it could drag on for bloody weeks.'

'Why do you say that?' Finch demanded. He had returned from his meeting with Nunn in a mood of elation, buoyed up by the realization that this could be a really big case, not one of the run-of-the-mill homicides following a drunken brawl between husband and wife on a Saturday night. Boyce's hangdog expression exasperated him. It deflated his own feeling of exhilaration at the thrill of the chase, an attitude of mind which, until the meeting with Nunn, he hadn't managed to rouse in himself. Trust Tom to pull out the bung on it, he thought irritably.

'If this bloke Garston's gone into hiding it could take weeks, even months, before he's found, if ever,' the Sergeant explained. 'Besides, the Yard's going to take all the kudos when the case is brought to trial. We'll be stuck with the leg-work and none of the praise. I can see it coming. Poor relations, that's what we are compared to the glamour boys at the Met.'

He probably was thinking of Munro, Finch thought. Munro had been a Metropolitan officer before he joined their force.

'Nunn will give credit where it's due,' he replied with more equanimity than he felt. 'Besides, there's no proof yet that Garston murdered Ray Chivers.'

Boyce held up three fingers, folding them down into the palm of his hand as he made each point.

'One: Garston's known to be violent. You said so yourself.

Second: he and Chivers were involved in a burglary and he knew Chivers had twenty-five thousand quid which has since disappeared. Third: he clobbered that policeman in the face and Chivers is found with his skull bashed in. I don't know what else you want.'

'Evidence, not theories,' Finch retorted sharply, 'and that's what I hope we'll get this afternoon when we interview Mr Aspinell. I want to find out exactly what information he's got that's so important he didn't want to pass it on to the duty constable. And while we're there, I also intend finding out why he pushed off just as I arrived. That bit doesn't make sense at all.'

8

Charlton Road, like Temperance Street, was a short, narrow turning of terraced cottages about ten minutes' walk from Holly Lodge, Finch estimated. In order to establish the distance between the two addresses, he had asked Boyce to make a detour and drive past the scene of the murder before drawing up outside Aspinell's house.

There was nothing to distinguish it from the others, Finch thought, running a speculative eye over the narrow brick façade as he waited for Boyce to join him on the pavement, although it was better kept than some of them, he added to himself, noting the brightly-polished door knocker on the green-painted front door, the crisp-looking net curtains which decently shrouded the front windows.

Boyce had said Aspinell was a widower; perhaps the old man was keeping up his dead wife's standards. Even the door-step and window-ledges had been whitened, a pretty pointless chore in the Chief Inspector's opinion, considering only a few feet of pavement separated the front of the house from the street.

As he knocked on the door, he was amused to notice that their arrival had already been observed by Aspinell's next-door neighbour. The curtain at the adjoining downstairs window was twitched aside and a woman's face appeared momentarily behind the glass before the curtain fell back into place.

Boyce nudged Finch with his elbow.

'That's the old biddy I spoke to yesterday. She evidently keeps an eye on what goes on in the street. Nothing better to do, I suppose,' he added as Finch knocked again.

If he hadn't been aware of the dark blur of the woman's face still watching them behind the net curtain, the Chief Inspector would have bent down to look through the letter-box. But it hardly seemed appropriate for a police officer of his rank.

'He's taking his time to answer,' Finch remarked, but before Boyce could speak, the neighbouring front door opened and the woman who had peered at them through the window appeared on the threshold. She was an elderly, grey-haired woman who walked with a stick. All the same, Finch thought, it hadn't taken her long to get from her front room to the door-step. For her age, she was still nippy on her feet.

'Are you wanting to see Mr Aspinell?' she asked and then, recognizing Boyce, she added, 'I know you, don't I? Aren't you the gentleman who called yesterday?'

'That's right,' Boyce replied. 'Isn't Mr Aspinell home yet?'

'Oh, yes. He came back last night about half past eleven. I heard the son-in-law's car. I sleep in the front, see, and could hear them talking as they went into the house. Not that Martin stayed all that long, not much above five minutes . . .'

'Mr Aspinell doesn't seem to be at home now,' Finch put in, cutting short the account. He had a vague premonition of disaster, nothing much, a mere flick of some intuitive nerve, like a tooth sending out a small signal of pain.

'Well, he ought to be. He's not gone out to my knowledge,' the woman replied, as if accused of some dereliction of duty.

'Is there a back entrance?' Finch asked sharply.

'Along the alley,' the woman said, pointing to an archway a few doors further down the street. 'But he never uses . . .'

Finch did not wait to hear the rest. Turning quickly on his heel, he set off at a rapid pace, Boyce, to whom some of the

Chief Inspector's anxiety had communicated itself, hurrying to keep up with him.

'What's the matter?' Boyce demanded. 'Do you think something's up?'

'God knows,' Finch replied.

Their voices echoed strangely in the long brick passageway which ran like a vault between the houses. Damp had darkened the brickwork in places and lay as a thin film of moisture over the cobblestones with which it was paved.

At the far end, it opened out into an alley, littered with old rubbish, which ran behind the walls of the backyards into which, at regular intervals, high wooden doors gave access.

Finch counted and at the fourth, paused and raised the latch. The yard door, painted the same green as the front, opened unwillingly and he had to lift it to stop it dragging on the concrete sill.

Beyond was a small garden, set with crazy-paving in the centre and with two narrow borders along each side, one which ran the full length of the yard to the back of the house, the other which stopped short at a one-storey addition, set at right angles to the rear façade and which Finch assumed housed the kitchen and the outside lavatory. Like the front of the house, the back was simple, with two sash windows, also net-curtained, and a back door which led into the single-storey addition. As in the front, there had been an attempt to keep up standards. The yard walls were whitewashed and covered with trellis against which climbing roses had been trained, while the borders, neatly weeded, contained the remnants of summer planting not yet killed off by the frost: lobelia, alyssum and forget-me-nots. A few bronze and yellow outdoor chrysanthemums, tied to stakes, were already in flower.

The back door was unlocked, as Finch found when he turned the handle, although he noticed that the curtains at the window over the sink were still drawn.

With one foot over the threshold, he paused to call out, 'Anyone at home?'

There was no answer.

Stepping inside and sweeping back the curtains to let in the light, he saw the kitchen was empty. It was neat, like the garden: everything in its place. A red plastic washing-up bowl was propped up in the sink to drain and a tea-towel hung on a little string line above it.

Boyce, going ahead of him into the living-room which led out of the kitchen stopped in the open doorway and swore quietly.

Finch said, 'What is it?' although he knew without being told what the Sergeant had found.

The body of an elderly man lay in front of the fireplace, its knees drawn up and the side of its face resting on the bright yellow and orange rays of the semi-circular hearthrug, meant to represent, Finch assumed, a rising or a setting sun.

The room was small and so crowded with furniture – two fireside armchairs as well as a dining-table and four upright chairs – that Finch had to step over the body and stand straddle-legged above it in order to get close enough to examine it.

From the position in which it was lying, it appeared that the man had been struck down from behind and had fallen forward on to his knees before slumping sideways. There was no need to guess at the cause of death. The shattered skull was only too horribly apparent, so, too, was the pool of blood which had darkened the bright sun-rays on the woollen rug.

The man was wearing pyjamas and a plaid dressing-gown, the sort that can be bought in many chain-stores – very similar, in fact, to the one which he himself owned, Finch realized, concentrating on its pattern in order not to identify too precisely the small white fragments which starred the edges of the wound. Bone, brain: God knows what exactly. He preferred not to look too closely.

'Stanley Aspinell?' Boyce asked behind him.

Finch straightened up and backed away, stepping gingerly to avoid a bedroom slipper which had come loose from one foot and lay by itself. The other had remained in place on the dead man's foot.

'Almost certain to be,' Finch replied, 'although we'll need an official identification.'

'Bang goes our witness,' the Sergeant continued with what

Finch thought was a particularly unfortunate choice of phrase even for Boyce. 'Do you want me to send for the team or will you do it?'

'You see to it, Tom,' he replied and, as Boyce left the room to report on the car radio, he realized that one of the experts who would make up their number would be Marion Greave. It was ironic, he thought with a wry grimace. Here he was, trying to put her out of his mind while the fates seemed to be conspiring to bring them together. And what a hell of a way to meet, over yet another dead body with a smashed-in skull!

Boyce came tramping back, coughing loudly, something he hadn't done until that moment. It occurred to Finch that his symptoms might be psychosomatic, a sign of stress. Glancing quickly at the Sergeant, Finch wondered if he hadn't been too hard on him and Boyce was under more strain than he had realized. He didn't want him cracking up at this point, for God's sake.

But the Sergeant's face contained his usual impassive expression.

'They're on their way,' he announced, adding, 'I wonder what happened to the dog?'

'What dog?' Finch demanded. He had forgotten its existence.

'The old bloke's. Didn't the desk constable say he had a dog with him when he called at headquarters?'

They found it behind one of the armchairs, huddled into the corner as if it had been trying to escape the same death which had overtaken its master, the legs stiffly extended in an attitude of running, the back of its head shattered like the old man's.

While they waited for the others to arrive, Finch made a quick tour of the house, opening doors and establishing the layout of the place as he had done at Holly Lodge. Not that there was much to inspect: a sitting-room which looked unused, a three-piece suite grouped stiffly; upstairs, a boxroom which had been converted into a bathroom and two bedrooms, the one in the front, like the sitting-room, appearing to be shut off although the heavily-veneered furniture and the double bed suggested it had once been the main bedroom.

Stanley Aspinell had slept in the smaller back bedroom in a single bed, the covers of which had been thrown back as if he had got up hurriedly. A dog's basket with a blanket folded in the bottom of it stood in one corner of the room.

Finch wondered which of them kept the other company, the man or the dog; or perhaps it was a shared companionship against the loneliness of the long night hours.

He heard McCallum and the others arrive and went downstairs to meet them, assigning them their tasks much as he had done at Holly Lodge – some to the scene of the murder, others to search the rest of the house and the backyard, while a group of uniformed men were sent off to make house-to-house inquiries of the neighbours. Munro, who was among the first to arrive, took charge of the upstairs rooms this time, Boyce the ground floor.

The tiny house seemed to reverberate to the sound of men's feet and voices and Finch thought wryly that the old man had probably never had so many visitors inside it at one time.

Would he have enjoyed the company? he wondered. Or would he have been distressed by the confusion they were creating among his neat, carefully tended possessions, the fingerprint powder spread on his furniture, his cupboards opened and searched?

He felt oddly distanced from it all as if the repetition of the same sequences of actions, already performed only the day before, had blunted his own susceptibilities and he was merely going through a routine which he knew too well.

Even the arrival of Marion Greave could not jolt him out of this mood. He let her in himself this time and showed her into the living-room. After that he forgot, or almost forgot, her existence although there flashed through his mind an image of her kneeling beside the body to probe delicately at the wound in the dead man's skull but, mercifully, before he could develop it too exactly, Boyce interrupted him.

He emerged from the sitting-room, carrying a small note-book, and announced, 'It's the old chap's address book. I found it in the sideboard drawer. There's an entry in it under Martin, Martin Southall, which could be the son-in-law's. I thought you would like to have it. The next of kin'll have to be told.'

'Yes, of course,' Finch said abstractedly, taking the book from him.

Still holding it, he walked out into the backyard where the three Detective Constables, their search of the area completed, were standing about.

Nothing of great significance had been found and Finch sent them off to extend their search into the alleyway.

When they had gone, he remained in the yard, grateful for the chance to be alone. There was nothing else he could contribute for the time being. The men knew their job and could be left to get on with it. His involvement would come later when all the separate threads of the inquiry would have to be drawn together, decisions made, new aspects of the investigation initiated.

He looked up at the sky. It was a typical late autumn day, lowering and with a hint already in it of the winter to come although a pale sun, diffused behind clouds, was bright enough to hurt his eyes when he stared directly at it. The bare branches of the trees in the neighbouring gardens and the lines and angles of the roofs and chimney pots which crowded close seemed incised against its watery brilliance.

Absorbed in his own thoughts, he was unaware of Marion Greave's arrival. She appeared suddenly at his side and, startled, he turned to see her regarding him gravely.

'Are you all right?' she asked.

He was touched by her concern but embarrassed by it as well, feeling that he had unwittingly betrayed to her a vulnerability which he would rather she had not seen.

'Just thinking,' he replied and added quickly, 'You've examined the body? It's murder, isn't it?'

'No question about that.'

They were talking easily and naturally as he and Pardoe might have done, two professionals using the kind of laconic speech which eschews any emotional response either to the subject itself or to themselves.

'And the same method?'

'As in the other case? It seems like it. I'll have to make a detailed examination to be certain but, yes, at first glance it would seem so.'

'Two deaths,' Finch said half to himself. 'Three, if you count the dog. He must have used the same tactics, too, calling at the house either late at night or early in the morning and battering his victims over the head when they least expected it. Someone plausible, therefore, not likely to arouse suspicion. Ray Chivers let him in, so did Stanley Aspinell. At least, there's no sign of a forced entry in either case so both victims must have got up to open the door.'

'Do you usually build up a mental picture of the murderer?' Marion Greave asked.

'It helps,' Finch replied. Odd, he thought, he no longer felt embarrassed. His normal reticence was disarmed by her cool, steady eyes which regarded him with genuine interest which few women, when talking to a man, were able to maintain for long, in his opinion. She seemed to expect nothing in return, neither the arousal of his own curiosity nor appreciation for her own.

'I can add a few details to that picture,' she told him. 'Almost certainly it's a man and someone tall and heavily-built – taller than either of his victims. In both cases, only one blow was struck and it was with a downward action.'

'Ray Chivers was five feet eleven.' Finch contributed this piece of information from his own recollection of the description of the wanted man.

'Then his murderer is at least that height, probably a couple of inches taller. Right-handed, too. Does that help?'

'It could,' Finch agreed. As he said it, he wondered if the description fitted Garston. 'What about the weapon? Was it metal? Flat or round-edged?'

He was thinking of the heavy spanner with which Garston had struck that policeman in Hampstead. But how in the hell had he known about Aspinell and where to find him?

'Sorry,' Marion Greave replied. 'I'll have to let you know. I hadn't finished the tests on the first victim when I was called out on this case. I'll be in touch with you as soon as I can – tomorrow probably. What's that you're holding?' she added.

Finch glanced at the small address book he was still carrying. It was covered in red imitation leather with the word 'Addresses' stamped on the front in gilt and looked like a birthday or Christmas present: the type of gift which someone, despairing of choosing something more personal, might send as safe and moderately acceptable. He had forgotten he was still holding it.

'It's Stanley Aspinell's,' he explained. 'Boyce found it. I'll have to get in touch with Aspinell's family. God, how I hate that part of the job!'

He spoke without thinking, some deep spring of anger and distaste suddenly released by the sight of the book. 'What the hell do you tell them?' he continued, turning his face away as he shoved the book into his pocket. ' "Sorry, I know your father was an old man and probably never did anyone any harm but all the same someone's bashed the back of his head in"?'

'Who are you taking with you?' Marion Greave asked. Her voice was calm, containing that kind but aloof tone which he imagined she would use on an overwrought patient. It occurred to him that in her job as a doctor she must have to face similar situations as himself, dealing with relatives after a death or, worse still, informing a patient that he had some terminal disease. He felt suddenly ashamed of his outburst.

'Boyce or Munro,' he replied. 'Probably Boyce. He has the right sort of face for coping with grief: kind but impassive. I've often thought he'd make a damned good undertaker.' Despite himself, a note of bitterness crept into his voice. 'And a WPC, of course. Aspinell had a daughter. He was baby-sitting for her last night.'

As he said it, he wondered if the murderer had been aware of this fact. Had he, like Boyce, called on Aspinell earlier in the evening and, finding him out, had returned later that night? The timing had to be fortuitous, however. He couldn't have known Aspinell had been to police headquarters as a potential witness. Or could he? Perhaps the crime was carefully planned after all so that Aspinell died before he could make a statement and pass on his evidence. And if that were the case, it suggested the killer had been following Aspinell's movements. Did that fit in with Garston? Finch wasn't sure. On the face of it, it seemed unlikely that an East End criminal would be hanging about Chelmsford, following an elderly man home. Nunn might know something of Garston's habits. Certainly the burglary in Hampstead had been carefully planned and the same attention to detail could have been extended to this back-street murder which appeared to have no possible motive except in relation to the murder of Ray Chivers and the London bobby. And in that case, he was dealing with no ordinary criminal but a man who was both ruthless and intelligent.

Marion Greave was saying, 'I've finished the preliminary examination. You can have the body moved whenever you want to.'

'Thanks,' Finch replied.

Now that their conversation was over, he felt his former embarrassment return and, as he escorted her back to the house and waited while she collected her coat and medical bag, he wondered what else he ought to say to her.

Sorry your Sunday's been disrupted? Or, Thank you for all you've done?

Neither seemed adequate or appropriate.

With Pardoe, he would have simply nodded his acknowledgement and walked away; two busy professional men parting with the minimum of social niceties, neither feeling the need to say anything at all.

She emerged into the hall, dressed in the long, fur-collared coat and looking, Finch thought, like a girl cossack.

Before he could open his mouth or get himself to the door, she had smiled and nodded to him without speaking and let herself out of the house. The front door shut briskly behind her.

Standing by the hall-stand, one of those ridiculous pieces of furniture which took up more room than its usefulness warranted, Finch suddenly burst out laughing, to the surprise of Munro who was coming down the stairs. It was a laugh of pure relief. He felt he had broken through some barrier in their relationship which had been entirely of his own making. From now on, he knew they would meet on an entirely different footing, on his part, that is, not hers. She had never been anything except herself. There would be no need for further embarrassment although he realized at the same time that he would still find it difficult to be completely frank with her except on a professional basis. Like a man surprised in the bath, he would still grab up the equivalent of a towel to hide his ultimate nakedness. Perhaps, in time, he'd learn to dispense with even that social cover.

Munro paused at the foot of the stairs, his full, dark eyes curious although he said nothing except, 'We've finished upstairs, sir. It looks as if Aspinell was in bed when his murderer called.'

'Yes, that's what I concluded,' Finch replied and felt a touch of mild exasperation at Munro's explicitness. Boyce had the same habit of pointing out the obvious, but without that faint air of superiority which Munro managed to convey. Looking at that positive face with its heavy eyebrows and moustache, Finch came to a decision.

'We should be finished down here as well shortly. We'll get the body moved and then I'll take Boyce with me to inform the next of kin. I'll leave you to finish up here. Make sure the house is locked and a PC is left on duty.' Pulling out the address book from his pocket, he turned the pages. 'If you want me, I'll be at 19 Claremont Avenue. That's on the Cavendish estate.'

'Very good, sir,' Munro replied. He sounded subdued as if aware of Finch's exasperation.

Perhaps he had his own sensitivity after all, Finch thought as, tramping down the hall, he shouted for Boyce.

9

The Cavendish estate was a new development on the outskirts of the town: small, red-brick houses and bungalows which, in their neat arrangement among tiny gardens and tree-lined roads, had the look of a toy-setting. Some child, with a build-it-yourself model kit, might have laid it out, including the parade of shops – a greengrocer's, a chemist's, a newsagent's cum post-office and a mini-supermarket with posters advertising 2p off baked beans pasted in the windows.

Claremont Avenue was close to the shops. Handy for Aspinell's daughter, Finch thought as they turned into the road. He had been silent on the drive there, Boyce at the wheel and the WPC in the back seat, who had caught his morose mood, hardly speaking either.

Number nineteen was a bungalow with an integral garage and new-looking rose trees in the front garden. An attractive, fair-haired young woman, slightly built like Aspinell, opened the door to them.

Finch preferred to forget the next quarter of an hour. The utter disbelief, followed by the shock and the outburst of grief were familiar to him but, all the same, he felt incompetent to deal with them. He was grateful when the WPC, a sensible, maternal woman although only in her early twenties, took charge of the wife and the children, a boy of six and a three-year-old toddler, and led them away. In the tiny bungalow, their combined cries could be heard, muffled by the intervening doors.

Which left Finch, Boyce and the husband, Martin Southall, alone in the living room which was scattered with children's toys and had the remains of tea still on the table.

'Sorry about the mess,' Southall said. It was an automatic apology. They were standing in an embarrassed group in the sitting-room end of the room where a three-piece suite was drawn up in front of a gas fire, turned on against the afternoon chill. Wedding photographs stood on the mantelshelf, one of a smiling bride and groom standing alone, the other of a group of friends and relatives clustered on the steps outside a church, Stanley Aspinell no doubt among them although Finch could not distinguish individual features among the twenty or so faces perched one above the other.

'Sit down,' Southall continued. His pleasant, slightly immature features seemed inadequate to express anything other than a harassed and uneasy concern as to what was expected of him in the circumstances.

As they lowered themselves on to the seats, Finch and Boyce taking an armchair each, Southall one end of the settee, some response seemed to be released in him.

'I still can't believe it,' he repeated. 'Who'd want to kill an old chap like that? He didn't have anything worth pinching in the house either.' Jerking his head towards the door from behind which his wife's grief was still audible, he added, 'She'll never get over it; thought the world of her dad. She was the youngest, see, and they made a lot of her at home. It was bad enough when her mum died. She lost a baby that time: miscarried at three months.'

He seemed bewildered, perhaps even a little resentful, at the effect of these family tragedies on his wife.

'Mr Aspinell had other children?' Finch asked.

'Yes,' Southall replied. 'Two more girls, older than Marilyn. Oh, Christ, I suppose I'll have to break the news to them.' He seemed plunged into gloom at the thought.

'I believe Mr Aspinell was baby-sitting for you last night,' Finch went on, turning to the subject in hand. He had told Southall and his wife very little about the circumstances surrounding the murder and both of them had assumed that Aspinell had been killed by an intruder, an impression that Finch was not eager yet to dispel. Until he had the full facts of the case and had established a definite connection with Ray Chivers' death, he preferred to leave the details blurred as far as the Southalls were concerned.

'That's right. I took Marilyn to the pictures. There was something she wanted to see at the Odeon. I picked her dad up about half past six and brought him here. Then me and Marilyn went out about quarter past seven. I suppose we got back just before eleven. I stopped to buy some fish-and-chip suppers and we ate them when we got home.'

He appeared to think that this recital of the previous evening's events was what Finch wanted because he looked surprised when the Chief Inspector asked, 'How did your father-in-law seem?'

'Seem? Much as usual. He hadn't a lot to say for himself, but then he never did. Marilyn's mother used to do most of the talking and I suppose dad got into the habit of keeping his mouth shut.'

'Did he say anything about a house in Temperance Street?'

'No, he didn't. Has this got anything to do with his murder?' Southall asked.

'Perhaps,' Finch said non-committally. 'It's a possible lead we're trying to follow up.'

Boyce put in his own pennyworth in contribution.

'There's just a chance there might be a witness,' he commented, his voice adding its imperturbable weight to Finch's. 'Somebody in a car?'

The slight upward inflection left the sentence dangling deliberately in the air.

'Car?' Southall repeated. 'Now you come to mention it, he did speak about a car. It's the first time he's ever shown an interest. On the way here from his house, he asked me what make I had. It's a Ford Escort, as a matter of fact. He wanted to know what make would be bigger than mine and I said, "Well, it would depend on whether it was British or foreign" and he said he didn't know except it was a dark colour. I pulled his leg a bit about it. "You thinking of buying yourself a motor?" I said. "If it's secondhand, let me give it the once-over first." I'm in the trade, see: a mechanic. You have to be careful with the secondhand trade. There's some dealers passing off rubbish as good quality vehicles. They do a quick respray, fiddle the mileometer and stick five hundred quid on the list price.'

It was obviously a subject on which he felt more at home than sudden death, and Finch had to lead him back to the point.

'What else did your father-in-law say?'

'About the car? Nothing much. He just said he wasn't thinking of buying one, that was all. He didn't speak of it again.'

'What time did he leave?' Boyce asked.

'Just before half past eleven. Like I said, we had a fish-and-chip supper, although dad didn't finish it. He said it was too late for him to eat much. Then I took him home. He could have stayed. He's spent the night here other times when we've been late home. The settee lets down into a bed. But last night he seemed keen to get back to his own place.' Southall paused before bursting out in a rare show of emotion, 'God, I wish now I'd made him stay! He'd still be alive, wouldn't he?'

'Possibly,' Finch agreed. 'Did he have the dog with him?'

'Yes, it went everywhere with him. Bloody animal! I hate dogs. It used to leave its hairs all over the carpet.' He shifted his feet to look down resentfully at the dark red carpet which covered that end of the room. As if in explanation of this sudden show of bitterness, he added, 'Marilyn used to go mad trying to hoover them up.'

'So it would have been about quarter to twelve when he got home?' Finch asked, ignoring the outburst, although he wondered just how far Southall's resentment was really directed at the dog and not at his father-in-law.

'Near enough. I went into the house with him for a few minutes. He'd remembered a shelf that wanted fixing and I said I'd bring my tools over when I could find the time.'

'Did he keep the back door locked when he was out of the house?' Finch asked.

'Yes, always. As a matter of fact, I saw him turn the key in it when I picked him up at half past six.'

'What about at night?' Boyce put in.

'He locked it before going to bed if it wasn't already fastened, especially since there's been these stories about teenagers breaking in and mugging old people. If I had my way, I'd string the lot of them up.'

Which would confirm, Finch thought, his own impression that Aspinell had got out of bed to let his murderer in. In the light of what Southall had just said regarding his father-in-law's caution over security, it made his action all the more incredible. What in hell had persuaded him to come downstairs and unlock the back door?

'What about the dog? Would it have barked?'

'Not when someone knocked. Dad had it trained not to. He thought it would be a nuisance to the neighbours to have it yapping. It'd have followed him downstairs though.'

'It did,' Finch said briefly. 'Whoever murdered your father-in-law killed the dog as well.'

Martin Southall had the grace to look shamefaced.

'Poor little blighter. I hope to God it went for whoever did it.'

Finch didn't want to explain that, judging by the position in which its body had been lying, it had done no such thing although, to give the creature its due, it might have arrived on the scene too late to attempt to rescue its master. It was an old dog. Finch couldn't imagine it could manage the stairs very quickly.

Glancing across at Boyce, he rose to his feet.

'That's all for the moment, Mr Southall. Thank you very much for your help.'

'I don't seem to have done much,' Southall admitted with a disarming and unexpected frankness.

'I'd like a statement from you later and we'll need someone to identify the body formally. Would you be willing?'

'Not willing but I'll do it,' Southall replied. 'I wouldn't want the wife . . . Oh, Christ!' he broke off and put a hand over his mouth.

'I'll send a car over for you later,' Finch said, turning away. 'We'll show ourselves out.'

The WPC met them in the hall where they talked together in low voices.

'I'll stay,' she said. 'I think a doctor ought to be with her. The next door neighbour's on the phone so I'll ring through when I've got the number from her husband.'

'Are you all right?' Finch asked. She looked dishevelled, her tunic unbuttoned and her hair flopping loose on her forehead.

A pretty girl, Finch thought. She'd make someone an excellent wife.

The same thought must have been in her mind because she smiled at him as she said, 'I've just got the kids to bed, sir. Good practice for later on when I have my own. I was just going to put the kettle on to make tea for Mrs Southall. Aren't you going to stay?'

Boyce looked eager but Finch turned down the offer.

'No thanks. We ought to be pushing off.'

'Why?' Boyce demanded as they left. 'We've finished at the

scene of the crime. Ten minutes wouldn't have made any difference.'

Finch was about to reply when he stopped short at the sight of Marion Greave getting out of a car which was parked just behind their own. Her presence there was so unexpected that he could think of nothing to say to her as she approached.

'There's the doctor,' Boyce announced, stating the obvious as usual. Aware of the Sergeant's curiosity, Finch motioned him to get into the car before stepping forward to intercept her before she came too close. 'Is something wrong?' he asked.

'Not really. I wanted to see if you were all right and to offer you a lift if you needed one. The Sergeant with the moustache gave me this address. He was still at the house in Charlton Road when I called back there.'

'Munro,' Finch said automatically. He was surprised and even a little secretly gratified to see that she had lost some of her normal composure and that, for once, it was she rather than him who showed signs of embarrassment. It pleased him also that she had gone to the trouble of discovering Southall's address and seeking him out although some of his pleasure was dampened by her next remark.

'I have a little more information which I thought you might need. That's really why I wanted to see you. Could you spare the time to come back to the surgery with me?'

'Now?' Finch asked and realized a second too late that it was hardly the most gallant of responses.

'If you can. It shouldn't take more than half an hour at the most and I can drive you back to headquarters afterwards.'

'Of course,' he said, trying to retrieve the situation. 'I'll just have a quick word with my Sergeant.'

Boyce looked up at him from the front seat of the car with a knowing expression as Finch explained the reason for Marion Greave's arrival.

'So I'll be back at headquarters later,' he concluded. 'Tell the others to wait. Meanwhile, you can get yourself that cup of tea in the canteen.'

He wanted to add, 'And take that stupid grin off your face,' but thought better of it.

'Boyce merely said demurely, 'Right, sir,' before driving off.

But Boyce's reaction seemed more accurate than Finch had imagined for, once inside Marion Greave's car, she confessed without any preliminaries, 'I wasn't being entirely frank with you. I had an ulterior motive in coming to find you.'

'Oh yes?' Finch said carefully and glanced sideways at her profile. She was looking straight ahead, small, firm, efficient hands holding the steering-wheel. Usually Finch felt uneasy when he was driven by a woman: a quite unreasonable, chauvinistic attitude, as he himself would have admitted. Nevertheless, he always kept one foot poised over an imaginary brake. With Marion Greave, he found no need for such a precaution. Her driving, like everything else she did, was skilful and competent.

She turned her head briefly to look at him, the little pouches under her eyes crinkling up.

'It's a purely professional interest,' she countered with amusement.

'Oh,' Finch replied, not knowing whether to be pleased or sorry.

'Seriously, though, as a doctor, I'm rather concerned about you. I thought you looked strained when we were talking a little earlier this afternoon. Have you had anything to eat today?'

'I had breakfast.'

'That's not good enough. I'll get you something while you're looking at some drawings I've done of the wound on Ray Chivers' skull. I asked your photographer, McCallum, to make some life-size close-up prints and . . . anyway, you'll see what I mean when you see them.'

Bright of her, Finch thought, and wondered what McCallum's attitude had been to her request, although if anyone showed interest in his work, he'd be prepared to stay up all night if necessary preparing prints. She certainly worked faster than Pardoe who hated to be rushed.

'He dropped the blow-ups at the house this afternoon,' Marion Greave continued, 'and I've been studying them since. I thought you might want to look at them and have half an hour's break at the same time. Have I presumed too much?'

'No, of course not,' Finch said promptly. With anybody else he might have been angry, but her frankness was disarming. All the same, a faint warning signal buzzed somewhere at the back of his mind. Marion Greave evidently liked having her own way, however altruistic her motives might be and however charmingly she might set about getting it.

Her house was in the Springfield area, in a short cul-de-sac of detached Edwardian houses, solid and respectable-looking. Hers was at the end, its rather plain, grey-brick façade with its formal sash windows softened by climbing roses and Virginia creeper. A single-storey, modern addition to the side of the house, with a separate door, was probably her surgery, Finch assumed.

She took him through the front door into a long hall, its walls covered with framed water colours, and from there into a large drawing room at the back of the house with a pair of glass doors looking out into an informal garden of trees and shrubs which gave the impression of a country rather than a suburban setting.

As he looked about him with quick, veiled glances, trying not to appear too curious, Finch's first reaction was that he might have expected the cool simplicity of the white walls and polished parquet floor, even the books which filled the floor to ceiling shelves along the whole of one wall.

What he had not anticipated were the colours. They glowed against the pale background from the rugs on the floor, the long curtains of lemon-coloured silk at the windows, the vases of yellow, red and bronze chrysanthemums and the pictures on the walls. One in particular caught his attention. It hung above the fireplace and even his untutored eye could tell it was a superb example of an eighteenth-century Dutch flower painting, its peonies, tulips and irises adding their own shades of rose, blue and amethyst to the general setting.

He felt strangely excited by the room. Normally, his physical surroundings meant little to him. His own house was conventionally furnished, mostly to the taste of his widowed sister who kept house for him. He had contributed nothing apart from his own books, a comfortable armchair and a workmanlike desk in the small spare bedroom which served him as an office.

But to walk into this room was like entering a jewelled box, full of objects to delight the eye, which was, at the same time, with its lamps and deep armchairs covered in green linen, a place to relax in.

Marion Greave had crossed to the fireplace and, taking an envelope which was propped up behind a silver-framed photograph, handed it to him.

'Here are the prints and drawings. Sit down and look at them while I get you something to eat. Would coffee and a sandwich suit you?'

'Perfectly,' Finch replied. He was about to add some politely conventional remark about not wanting to put her to any trouble, but she had already left the room.

Before turning away to sit down, Finch took a second look at the photograph which stood on the mantelpiece and to which his attention had been drawn as she had taken the envelope from behind it. It was of a young man, standing easy and relaxed with his hands in his pockets against a background of leaves, laughing into the camera.

Finch studied the features. He was dark-haired and, while not exactly handsome, possessed that air of confidence and self-possession which often passes for good looks. Finch certainly couldn't imagine him feeling ill at ease and he felt a surge of unexpected envy towards the young man for his self-confidence and also for his possible relationship with Marion Greave.

Was he a friend or a lover? There was no way of knowing except by means of a direct question which Finch realized he was hardly in a position to ask. His own relationship with Marion Greave made so personal an approach impossible. All the same, it suddenly seemed terribly important to him to know, otherwise . . .

Otherwise, what? he asked himself, turning his back on the photograph and seating himself on one of the armchairs.

Even he wasn't sure of the answer and, deliberately shutting his mind to the problem, he switched his attention to the contents of the envelope.

They were self-explicit, comprising a series of life-size close-ups of the fractured skull over which thin sheets of paper had been laid. On to these the edges of the wound had been drawn in with a fine ink line. The photographs had been taken from several angles and demonstrated quite clearly the shape of the wound.

One single blow, Marion Greave had said, and that much was obvious from both the drawings and the prints.

What he was less sure about was the type of weapon which could have caused the fracture. As he sat studying the photographs and tracings, Marion Greave returned to the room, carrying a tray.

She had said a sandwich, but what she offered him was no mere snack, more a meal in itself. It was a triple-decker of finely-cut rye bread and contained, as Finch discovered when he bit appreciatively into it, salami, lettuce, tomato, sliced black olives and some kind of spicy dressing. The coffee was fresh and scalding hot.

Having poured herself a coffee and drawn another chair close to Finch's, Marion Greave took the prints and drawings from the Chief Inspector and pointed out the details to him as he chewed his way through the mammoth sandwich, nodding speechlessly as she made each point.

'A single blow struck downwards, as I explained to you this morning. These close-ups show that particular effect quite clearly. But in this one,' and here she shuffled the prints so that the third one was now uppermost, 'you can see the actual shape of the fracture. When I spoke to you earlier, I'd only had time to glance at the prints so I couldn't be sure. But I've since examined them more carefully and I'm absolutely certain now that the weapon which made this wound was something heavy, smooth and round-headed, not sharp or angled such as the edge of an iron bar.'

'Could it have been a spanner?' Finch asked, swallowing hastily.

'No.' She sounded quite positive. 'A spanner's flat on one surface although the head of it is rounded. But it's too thin to cause this type of wound. I'd say the weapon you are looking for is shaped like a baseball bat, only smaller.'

'A cosh?' Finch suggested.

'That's possible. I'm no expert on coshes but provided the shape fits the description, yes, it could be a cosh. But it would be a professional weapon, not a home-made one.'

'Why do you say that?'

'The head of it that was used to bludgeon Ray Chivers to death was smooth, as I've already said. This afternoon, I looked at some of the hairs and flesh round the wound under the microscope and I couldn't find any wood fibres or particles of metal, rust or even dirt. This suggests it wasn't a roughly made weapon. Of course, forensic may discover something I've missed – after all, their labs are much better equipped than mine – but I'll bet you anything you like to name that it was a heavy, round-headed weapon, as I've described it, factory-made, not put together in someone's shed or picked up on a building site.'

Hoping to God he wouldn't bungle it, Finch said, 'I won't accept the bet but, if you're right, I'll take you out to dinner one evening.'

He seemed to have struck the right note for the little, smiling crinkles re-appeared under Marion Greave's eyes.

'I'll remind you of the offer when I'm proved right.'

'And now I ought to go,' Finch continued, putting down his empty plate and cup. It seemed a good idea to leave while he was on a winning streak. 'I've got reports to collect from a lot of rather tired detectives once I've rooted them out of the canteen. Which reminds me. I've some information which could help you in establishing the time of Aspinell's death. According to his son-in-law, he had a fish-and-chip supper at about a quarter to eleven last night.'

'Yes, that will be useful when I come to do the PM. If you're ready, then I'll run you back to headquarters.'

Finch picked up the reference in the car, his curiosity having got the better of him.

'Do you mind if I ask you something? What made you take up medicine, particularly pathology, in the first place?'

'You think it's unsuitable for a woman?' Marion Greave countered.

'Oh, no, not at all,' Finch lied quickly.

She was silent for a moment as if weighing up how much to tell him.

'I had an older brother I was very fond of. He was at King's studying pathology when he was killed in a car accident; one of those stupid, totally unnecessary deaths. I was in the sixth form at the time, intending to take up medicine but I chose to specialize in pathology to compensate for his death, I suppose. You may have noticed his photograph on the mantelpiece.'

'Yes, I believe I did,' Finch replied, trying to keep his voice steady. 'I'm sorry about his death.'

'It was years ago and anyway I got sidetracked into general practice. There aren't that number of posts going for women pathologists although I like to keep my hand in when I can. A lot of men feel it's a male occupation. It's extraordinary the amount of prejudice there still is in some professions.'

'I can imagine,' Finch murmured, feeling guilty about his own chauvinistic tendencies.

She may not have been entirely convinced by his remark for, as they drew up outside divisional headquarters, she remarked, 'As a mere woman doctor, may I give you a piece of advice? Don't overdo it. Chief Inspectors get tired as well as Detective Constables.'

He ducked down to look at her through the driver's window.

'I'll try to remember. Thanks for everything.'

He meant it to refer to more than the meal or the lift back, although he hoped she wouldn't read too much into it and, as he mounted the steps into the building, he was careful not to look back as her car drew away. Luck was one thing but some innate caution warned him against pushing it too far, although he wished to God he had the kind of temperament which allowed him to plunge in without this fear of commitment or the dread of making a fool of himself.

In consequence, he was snappy with Boyce when the Sergeant knocked and entered his office, wearing the same inane grin he had outside Southall's when Marion Greave had first approached them.

'Everything all right?' he asked nosily.

123

'Why shouldn't it be?' Finch demanded. He was shoving paper into a box file which he had labelled 'Stanley Aspinell' and, as Boyce hesitated on the other side of the desk, he added, 'Well, don't just stand there. Start getting the men organized. I'll see Kyle first. And get Munro up here as well. He ought to be in on the conference.'

Boyce retreated, closing the door carefully behind him.

It was interesting, Finch thought later, his exasperation a little tempered by amusement, to see how the two Sergeants arranged their chairs when they settled themselves in his office, Boyce claiming the seat next to the desk and pulling it slightly forward so that it gained precedence over Munro's while Munro drew his towards the centre so that he was directly facing the Chief Inspector. Their actions reminded him that he had still done nothing to resolve the situation between the two men. For his part, Munro seemed less aware of the significance of the seating arrangements than Boyce and sat back comfortably, crossing his legs, his notebook at the ready and with that alert expression on his face which, for some unaccountable reason, Finch found almost as annoying as Boyce's habit of clearing his throat as he sat down.

Perhaps Marion Greave is right, he thought, and I do need to take things more easily. Certainly, his threshold of tolerance seemed considerably lower than normal.

Kyle gave his verbal report first. He had been in London all day, returning in time to take part in the Charlton Road investigation and he, too, looked tired, his pleasant nondescript features made even more indefinite by fatigue.

What he had to report was, however, useful. He had interviewed Fuller, the landlord of Holly Lodge, who had confirmed that the house had been let on a month's lease on the previous Wednesday, three days before the discovery of Ray Chivers' murder. Someone had rung him up, asking for a letting on any property outside London and Fuller had suggested Holly Lodge which was empty at the time. The same afternoon a man had called at the office to collect the key and had paid in cash.

'Description?' Finch demanded.

Kyle flapped over the pages of his notebook.

'In his late twenties, sir. About five feet nine; slightly-built; black hair; thin features. Gave the name of John Smith.' Despite his fatigue, Kyle managed a smile. 'I got the impression Fuller wasn't too bothered who his client was. It was the money he was more interested in. While I was in the area I made a few more inquiries. It seems Fuller owns quite a lot of East End property as well as houses in Romford and Chelmsford.'

Which confirmed as well as extended the information they already had on Fuller, Finch thought. As he jotted down the details, he remembered Nunn's description of Benny Costello, Ray Chivers' flat-mate, which it seemed to match and which he'd have to check with the Chief Superintendent as soon as possible.

'Anything else?' he asked.

'No, that's the lot, sir,' Kyle replied.

'Then push off home,' Finch told him. 'You've done enough for one day.'

After Kyle's evidence, the rest of the reports didn't amount to much. The search of the yard and alleyway – negative; the interviews with Aspinell's neighbours – also negative. No one had seen or heard anything either that morning or the previous night. No car, no stranger, no noise – not even the dog barking.

'So that's that,' Finch announced as the last officer left the room, 'although it confirms what I'd already suspected. Whoever killed Aspinell was damned careful and also very plausible otherwise the old man wouldn't have let him into the house.'

'Could he have been known to Aspinell?' Munro asked.

'It's a possibility we ought to bear in mind,' Finch agreed, aware that, as Munro spoke, Boyce had deliberately creaked his chair as if disparaging Munro's comment. 'Any results yet on the inquiries round the shops from the Chivers' investigation?' he added.

'Not a lot yet, sir,' Munro admitted. 'He was certainly seen in the local pub, the Carpenters' Arms, and in the fish-and-chip shop on the corner of Trafalgar Street. I'm still checking out the town centre. Judging by the paper bags I found in that box of rubbish, he'd bought something at a men's outfitters as well as stuff from Woolworth's.'

'Get that checked as soon as you can,' Finch told him. 'And speaking of shops, I want the furniture traced. It looks new and the chances are it was bought recently. Make a note of those numbers stuck on the frames, by the way. They could be useful. Check the local shops first and, if nothing turns up, then try London. Chivers was from London and it's possible the stuff was bought there. Organize it between yourselves and use as many men as can be spared from the other inquiries.'

Boyce was about to speak when the ringing of the telephone forestalled him.

Picking up the receiver, Finch heard Nunn's voice, crackling with excitement, at the other end of the line.

'Listen, Jack! We've traced Garston to a caravan site on the Essex coast. We'll be moving in at dawn tomorrow morning to pick him up. Are you interested in being in on the kill?'

'Count me in! I wouldn't miss it for a thousand quid,' Finch replied, catching Nunn's mood of jubilation.

'You're on, cobber,' Nunn told him in mock Australian. 'I'll pick you up at your house at half past four.'

So much for Marion Greave's advice to take things easy, Finch thought, as he replaced the receiver.

10

It was still dark when Nunn collected Finch the following morning, although the street lamps were beginning to look pallid. As they drove through the town centre, as deserted as a city struck by plague, and headed towards the A12 Nunn gave the Chief Inspector an account of the background to the operation.

'It was the name of that landlord you gave me, Fuller, which first put us on to it. We checked him out yesterday afternoon and discovered he owned a lot more property than just a few houses in Chelmsford.'

'I know. One of my own men made similar inquiries,' Finch put in, instantly partisan.

'Among which,' Nunn continued, ignoring the interpolation, 'were some caravans at Bradham on the coast not far from Clacton. We put the squeeze on Fuller and he admitted letting one of them to a man answering Garston's description. Two of my men did an undercover recce down there yesterday and it's Garston all right. He's holed up there with some boyfriend. We thought we'd move in early before they're up and have time to know what's hit them.'

'I've got a description for you,' Finch countered. 'It's the man who rented the house in Temperance Street.'

As he finished repeating the details which Kyle had given him, Nunn said, 'That's Benny Costello, by the sound of it.'

'So he knew where to find Ray Chivers,' Finch pointed out.

'Or it's possible Garston could have got the same information either from Fuller, although he's not admitted to it, or from any of his East End contacts. That lot sticks together like gum on a carpet.'

Finch, who had already given Nunn a brief summary of the second murder, Aspinell's, continued, 'As both victims had their heads smashed in, I suppose Garston's a likely suspect.'

'It's certainly his style,' Nunn agreed.

'But how would he know Aspinell was a potential witness in the Chivers' case?'

'I wouldn't put anything past Garston. He's a bright lad and he had a lot to lose. And he's not only clever, he's got nerve as well – a gambler by instinct. Once he realized Aspinell had seen him, he could have followed him to headquarters and then home. Later on, he'd take the first chance he could to get rid of him.'

'There was a crowd hanging about the gate at Holly Lodge,' Finch admitted.

He tried to picture individual faces but realized it was an impossible task.

It would be ironic, he thought, if all the time Garston had been there with a police officer on duty and plain-clothes detectives, including himself, passing in and out of the house within feet of him. But, as Nunn had said, the man had nerve.

'As for persuading Aspinell to let him in,' Nunn added, 'don't forget he'd pulled much the same trick on Mitchell on the Hampstead job.'

'A policeman in uniform!' Finch exclaimed.

'Exactly. As far as we know, he still has the outfit, the cheeky bugger.'

There was a note of angry admiration in Nunn's voice.

'So he could have gone to Aspinell's house posing as a policeman. As Aspinell had already called at headquarters, he wouldn't have been suspicious. That's why he came downstairs and let him in.' Another thought struck Finch. 'But Aspinell didn't know we had his address. We got it from Beach, that friend of his.'

Nunn brushed the objection aside.

'Oh, that wouldn't worry Garston. He'd come up with some yarn. I told you, he's bright.'

Finch fell silent. The theory hung together but he still wasn't totally convinced that it was the right one. A lingering doubt remained that it was almost too plausible. It left no room for human error or just plain bad luck which, in his experience, bedevilled even the most carefully calculated plans: sod's law, in other words.

Of course, he'd find out soon enough once Garston was arrested, providing the man was prepared to make a complete statement.

Dawn, if you could call the faint lifting of the darkness into a pervading grey gloom anything so poetic, came as they entered the small town of Bradham, its shops still shuttered. The caravan site was a mile away, down a concrete road which led under a high wooden arch bearing, in peeling letters, the words 'Welcome to Sunnidays Holiday Park. Fun for the Whole Family'.

Ramps, called sleeping policemen, a quite inappropriate phrase, in Finch's opinion, spanned the road at intervals and slowed down their speed to ten miles an hour.

The countryside was flat, the sky taking up three quarters of the vista, the land a mere low plain of coarse grass cut about by drainage ditches. It looked sour as if the salt wind had sucked all the goodness out of it and the few trees which broke the monotonous skyline were crippled and bent sideways by the winter gales. To their left, the high escarpment of the sea wall, looking like part of a fortification, blocked out a view of the sea although steep steps leading up it gave holidaymakers access to the dubious pleasures of a beach facing the North Sea. Immediately opposite it were the first signs of the caravan site: a shop and a bingo hall, their windows boarded over and their doors padlocked. Beyond stretched the caravans themselves, row upon row, each on its own concrete base and with enough worn grass round it for a car to be parked or a couple of deck chairs to be set up.

'God!' Nunn exclaimed at the sight of it as he drew his car off the road behind the bingo hall to join the other vehicles already parked there.

Finch grinned.

'You should see it in the summer.'

'No thanks,' Nunn retorted. 'This is quite enough for me.'

They got out to greet a small huddle of men who were sheltering from a cruel, little breeze, as sharp as a blade, which came slicing in from the sea. As a defence, the wall seemed to serve only part of its function. It might keep out the high winter tides but the wind simply shouldered its way over it.

'You know the set-up,' Nunn said briskly, once he had introduced Finch to the men. 'We move in at 6 a.m. promptly. And there's no need for any rough stuff. I want Garston and his boyfriend picked up clean and then taken in separate cars to the station in Bradham. I've arranged for them to be questioned there before we ship them back to London.' Turning to Finch, he added, 'You'll want to be in on the interviews?'

'I'd like to,' Finch replied.

'Right.' Nunn checked his watch. 'We've got a quarter of an hour before we grab them. Any questions? No? Then I want you,' pointing to two plain-clothes men, 'to make the first move as we planned it yesterday. Nothing heroic or clever. Just knock at the caravan door and when it's opened, go straight in – no messing. I don't think Garston's armed but remember he could be. The rest of you spread yourselves out undercover and be ready to jump for it as soon as that door's opened. And no talking. I'll have the hide off any man who so much as opens his mouth.'

They set off at five minutes to six, the men taking separate routes between the rows of caravans, using them as cover for their movements.

Only a few of the vans were occupied, Finch noticed, as he followed behind Nunn. Most of them appeared to be empty.

They halted in a side turning, inappropriately named Beach View, where Nunn pointed out a caravan standing two berths away.

'That's Garston's,' he whispered.

It was a large van with a window occupying the whole end wall facing them. Curtains of flowered material were drawn across it. A Mercedes looking incongruous in such a setting was parked beside it, well back, luckily, so that they had a clear view of the van door.

As they waited, the two men assigned to the task of making the initial move came into sight along the road, walking casually.

Beside him, Finch felt Nunn tense with excitement and he found his own chest muscles tighten as he watched them approach the caravan and, mounting the steps, knock loudly on the door. The delay while it was answered was almost unbearable. Then Finch saw the door open and the figure of a man appear: not Garston, he thought. This man was young and blond, dressed in what appeared to be a short blue dressing-gown which barely covered his knees.

The detectives spoke to him although they were too far away for Finch to hear what was said. He saw the young man turn back towards the interior of the caravan as the two men began to shoulder their way past him. At the same time, the other plain-clothes and uniformed men began moving rapidly from their places of concealment behind the other vans. Nunn, giving Finch a look of pure joy, also stepped forward.

What happened next was so unexpected and bewildering that, for a few seconds, neither Finch nor the others seemed capable of grasping its significance.

The large window at the end of the caravan suddenly burst apart as if an explosion had shattered the glass, hurtling it forwards. A shape leapt down with it, fell to the grass and righted itself – a man, Finch realized as the figure crouched there momentarily. The next instant, he had bounded to his feet and raced off like a hare.

'Garston!' Nunn bellowed.

The men whirled about and gave chase, Nunn and Finch with them.

Garston had evidently intended to cut diagonally across the site where he might easily have been lost among the parked caravans, but two uniformed officers, quicker off the mark than the others, circled round to left and right, running parallel with him and forcing him to keep to the road. At the end, the sea wall blocked his escape where, after a moment's hesitation when he visibly faltered, he quickly recovered himself and, making for the steps, disappeared over the top.

As he pounded after him, Finch found himself admiring, however grudgingly, Garston's courage. A lesser man, realizing the odds were stacked against him, would have given up at the foot of the steps.

Topping the sea wall himself, he had an elevated view of Garston's final capture. The sand impeded his progress as well as the detectives' in pursuit of him so that the chase took on the dreamlike quality of a slowed-down film, arms and legs pumping in a ponderous frenzy. Behind the sluggishly fleeing figures, a sullen grey sea gathered itself up before heaving reluctantly forward with the same heavy motion, breaking finally in low, white-tipped rollers along the edge of the beach. The sky was the same colour as the water so that the scene seemed to consist of one flat, grey wash, only a line of liquid light separating the two elements.

They brought him down at the sea's edge in a flurry of water and sand out of which an arm was suddenly flourished before it disappeared into the mêlée, reminding Finch of the poem 'Not waving but drowning'.

There was something primitive about the capture as well as

poignant: the primeval struggle between the hunter and the hunted. Or perhaps it was even more primordial than that: the age-old combat between good and evil, an image which was dispelled as the two officers, wet through and swearing volubly, dragged Garston between them up the sea wall and down the other side. Garston, head low, feet dragging, hardly personified evil either, an impression Finch was to modify partly when later he confronted the man in an interview room at Bradham police station.

He had had time to recover and, although divested of his wet clothes and draped in a blanket, not a covering to lend much dignity to a man, he still managed to convey a sense of powerful personality. Part of it was sheer physical bulk. He was broad-shouldered and in his early thirties, with the type of face which immediately caught the attention, however unwilling, so that Finch found himself concentrating on the larger-than-average features, the wide forehead and full sensual mouth and chin which showed signs of good living, although the flesh was firm like the rest of his body. Garston might be self-indulgent but there was discipline there and, Finch suspected, a will of iron. The packed muscles in his bare forearms, folded across the top of the blanket, suggested a superb physical condition. In comparison, the young six-foot tall PC on duty inside the interview room looked a mediocre specimen of manhood.

Nunn dismissed him with a nod as he and Finch entered and, drawing up two straight-backed chairs, seated themselves opposite Garston on the other side of the table.

The Chief Superintendent began in a low-keyed conversational manner, quite different from his usual rapid, eager style of delivery, although Finch who knew him well, guessed that, under the easy manner, Nunn was simmering with excitement.

'Frank Garston?' Nunn began and the man, who had merely glowered at them as they entered, admitted this much with a brief jerk of his head.

It was about all he was willing to admit. As Nunn went over the details of the Hampstead burglary and the murder of PC Flower, Garston either remained silent or responded with the words, 'Where's your proof?'

Even Nunn's rejoinder, 'We've got Webber. He's made a statement about the part you and Ray Chivers played,' couldn't shake him.

'He's been verballed,' Garston retorted. 'Some clever sod of a detective's written it down for him and Webber's been forced to sign. I've got an alibi for that Thursday night; five people are prepared to swear I was in the club all evening.'

It was said in a bored voice as if Garston found the whole business of the interview a tedious waste of time, an attitude which Finch found more exasperating than if the man had lost his temper. He wondered how Nunn would react but the Chief Superintendent merely plodded on with the questioning in the same even voice.

As opponents, they were well-matched, Finch thought. Both men were experts in their own fields, Nunn on one side of the law, Garston on the other.

It was only as the first part of the interview ended that Nunn allowed himself to show his anger. As Garston repeated yet again, 'Where's your proof?' Nunn snapped back, 'You'll find out in court, Garston.'

It was a mistake. Garston smiled at the rejoinder, pleased at having stung Nunn into a reaction.

Flinging himself back in the chair, Nunn signalled to Finch to take up the questioning.

Finch had sat silent during Nunn's cross-examination, his expression deliberately bland. Several times he had seen Garston look across at him as if puzzled at his presence in the room and this knowledge gave Finch a psychological advantage as he began his own questioning.

'You know Ray Chivers, I believe?'

'Yeah, like I told him,' Garston replied, jerking his head at Nunn, 'I met Ray several times down the club I run in Bermondsey.'

He sounded off-hand as if he thought that the interview with Finch was going to be a mere reiteration of the same questions Nunn had put to him.

'A pleasant young man?' Finch suggested.

Garston hesitated as if suspecting a trap.

'He's all right, I suppose,' he said at last. 'I don't know him all that well.'

'And of course you haven't seen him for the past week?'

Again Garston paused, trying to work out the significance behind the question. Having denied, when Nunn questioned him, any knowledge of the Hampstead burglary or of Ray Chivers' part in it, he clearly felt uneasy about admitting how much he knew of Chivers' subsequent movements.

'I'm not sure. I don't take all that much notice of who's in the club some evenings.'

Finch remained silent, an old interviewing trick of his, allowing the silence to continue until even Nunn began to fidget. At last, Garston added, 'Come to think of it, someone did mention they hadn't seen him recently.'

'Had he moved on?' Finch asked. 'Found a new address?'

'I wouldn't know.' Garston refolded his arms as if to prevent himself from giving any more away.

'But I understand he's a friend of yours.'

'I told you, I know him; that's all.'

'As a club member?' Taking Garston's silence for agreement, Finch went on, 'People chat in clubs. That's part of their function – somewhere to meet friends for a drink and a talk. What's the gossip on Ray Chivers?'

The remark was intended to be disarming, even naïve, and Garston looked amused.

'Not a lot. He's got a live-in lover, Benny Costello, although, according to the chit-chat, he picked up with a new boyfriend a few months ago.'

This was news to both Finch and Nunn but neither man showed any reaction, Finch merely asking casually, 'Isn't that someone called Dave from Hoxton?'

Garston fell for it. Like most men with an over-developed sense of their own importance, he couldn't resist the opportunity to put someone right, especially a policeman.

'Then you've heard wrong,' he said in a jeering voice. 'According to my info down the club, it's some rich geezer, high up in the Civil Service. Ray meets him up the West End somewhere.'

'Sorry,' Finch said, sounding humble. 'I've got it wrong. You don't happen to know his name?'

'I don't,' Garston replied. 'I'd pass it on if I did.'

Finch believed him. Garston look gratified at having scored the one point as he thought. He wouldn't pass up the chance of scoring another.

This information, extracted from Garston without him being aware of it, could be important, Finch realized. It added another possible suspect to the list of those already compiled: Benny Costello and Garston himself.

Meanwhile, it was time for a change of tactics. Garston had now been sufficiently lulled into thinking that the man who faced him across the table with his bluff features and rather rambling manner was nothing more than a hick plain-clothes detective from somewhere out in the sticks.

'What were you doing last Friday night?' Finch snapped out suddenly.

'I was in the caravan,' Garston replied. He seemed taken aback by the abrupt change of manner.

'And Saturday night?'

'The same. What's all this about anyway?'

Garston looked aggrieved as if he resented this new line of questioning.

'Where's your proof?'

It was a word for word repetition of the phrase Garston had used on Nunn and Finch saw Nunn put his hand up to his mouth to hide a smile.

For the first time since the interview had begun, Garston seemed aware that he had lost control of the situation.

'Proof?' he demanded furiously. 'Why should I want to prove anything, for Christ's sake?'

'Because you may need an alibi,' Finch told him.

'Alibi to what? Are you trying to set me up? What the hell am I supposed to have done? Another robbery?'

'Another murder,' Finch said quietly, 'Two, in fact.'

'Jesus!' Garston said softly and sat back in his chair as if he had been struck in the face.

'So an alibi covering those two nights would be useful to us.

And to you.' Finch added the last remark as a mild after-thought.

'There's Terry,' Garston said. 'He'll vouch for me. You ask him. He'll tell you I wasn't out either evening.'

Finch got to his feet.

'We'll just check with him then, shall we?'

Nodding affably to Garston, he left the room, Nunn accompanying him and both men ignoring Garston's shouted demands.

'I want to see my solicitor! Do you hear me? I know my rights! You're trying to bloody frame me. Frigging police . . . '

The door closed on the last comment.

Outside in the corridor, Nunn grasped Finch's arm.

'My God, we've got him running! And thanks mainly to you, Jack. I never thought I'd see Garston go to pieces like that. I reckon he's almost in the bag. Lover-boy's going to be a push-over. He's a rabbit compared to matey in there.'

Terry, or to give him his full name, Terence Leonard Bentley, was waiting for them in another interview room. While the pursuit of Garston had been taking place, he had been arrested by two plain-clothes men who had remained behind and he had been allowed to dress before being taken to Bradham in a separate police car.

Wearing tight jeans and a pink shirt, unbuttoned at the neck, he jumped nervously to his feet as Nunn and Finch entered.

'Sit down,' Nunn told him. He had acquired a sheaf of official-looking papers from the desk Sergeant and, without looking at Bentley, proceeded to study them before spreading them out on the table. Finch, amused at the ploy, one he had used himself on many occasions, took the opportunity to study Bentley as, like the rabbit Nunn had compared him to, he watched with an expression of frightened fascination the Chief Superintendent's preparations.

He was younger than Finch had thought from the brief glimpse he had caught of him in the caravan doorway and good-looking in a sulky, slack-featured way. His hair, crisply-curled and blond, was too good to be true, Finch decided, noting at the same time the three studs, one a small, solitaire diamond, which decorated the whole side of one ear, and the gold chain round his neck. What was on the end of it was hidden under his shirt. Remembering the similar chain round Ray Chivers' neck, Finch wondered if it carried a St Christopher medallion and whether both pendants were not gifts from Frank Garston.

'Right!' Nunn said briskly. 'Name?'

Bentley repeated it and Nunn noted it down although Finch, from his side of the table, was able to see he had written an indecipherable scrawl on the top sheet of paper. The serious business of taking a statement would come later once Bentley and Garston were back in London on Nunn's patch.

'Age?' Nunn continued.

'Eighteen,' Bentley replied. He had a slight Midlands accent overlaid with a huskiness which Finch guessed was probably cultivated in order to give his voice a certain throaty charm.

Nunn flung down his pen in a pretended gesture of impatience.

'Come off it, lad! I've sorted out more juvenile delinquents than you've had hot dinners. What are you? Fourteen? Fifteen?'

'Fourteen and a half, nearly fifteen,' the boy said sullenly.

'And your address? And I don't want Frank Garston's. I mean where your parents live.'

'Kinderly.'

'Never heard of it,' Nunn said.

'No one has,' the boy replied resentfully. 'It's a dump just outside Manchester, miles from anywhere. And I'm not going back there.'

'So you've come down south to London, looking for the bright lights, eh?' Nunn suggested. 'And you've certainly found them – on a caravan site with Garston.'

His voice was full of an amused, pitying contempt.

'I'm not complaining,' Bentley replied with a flash of bravado.

'Don't be cheeky with me, sonny,' Nunn told him cheerfully. He might have been addressing his own teenage son. 'Tell me, how did you get mixed up with Frankie?'

'I met him about a week ago at the club he runs. A friend I'm kipping down with took me there. Then a few days later, this friend said, Would I fancy joining Frank? He'd got this caravan by the seaside. It sounded all right, so I said yes.'

'One of Frank's pimps, I shouldn't wonder,' Nunn said, addressing Finch. Seeing the look on the boy's face, he turned back to him in explanation. 'A pimp, sonny: someone who procures women or, in your case boys, for immoral purposes. Don't you realize you're Frank's little play-mate of the month just in case he got bored stuck down on the east coast on his ownsome? What do you know about him?'

'Nothing much.' The huskiness had gone and the boy's voice was shrill. 'He said he was in trouble but he didn't say nothing about the police. He told me it was a gang out after him, something to do with his clubs, and he wanted to lie low until things got sorted.'

'Heard of the Hampstead burglary?' Nunn asked. 'Or PC Flower?'

The boy's bewilderment couldn't be anything but genuine and Nunn after staring him in the face for several seconds, turned to Finch, making a dismissive gesture as much as to say, He's all yours.

'Let's go back to last Friday and Saturday,' Finch began, his voice avuncular, although in this case it wasn't entirely assumed. 'What did you and Garston do on those evenings?'

'Nothing much. We watched telly.'

'Did either of you go out at all?'

'Yes, Frankie did.'

'Which evening?' Finch asked, trying not to sound too eager.

'Both Friday and Saturday,' Bentley replied. He seemed less sure of himself now that Finch had taken over the questioning, more child-like both in voice and manner.

'Where did he go?'

'Where he always went: down the fish-and-chip shop in Bradham. Oh, I forgot, he went to the boozer as well on Friday. He brought back a bottle of vodka with the fish and chips.'

In the same way in which he had disguised his eagerness, Finch now hid his disappointment.

'How long was he gone altogether?'

'About half an hour, maybe three quarters.'

'And that was all? He didn't go out again?'

The boy shook his head.

'Could he have left the caravan later on those nights without you knowing?'

'No.' Bentley sounded quite positive.

'Why are you so sure?' Finch demanded.

Bentley blushed, the colour running up his cheeks and forehead.

'I just am.'

Nunn laughed, as much at Finch's naïvety as at the boy's embarrassment.'

'They were bunking in together, that's why.' As the boy hung his head, Nunn continued, addressing him directly, 'But all the same you're lying about Garston, aren't you? He put you up to it so that he'd have an alibi for those two nights.'

'It's the truth!' Bentley retorted, lifting his head and looking defiantly at Nunn.

'Look, lad,' Nunn said, resuming his reasonable, I'm-doing-this-for-your-own-good tone of voice, 'you're in enough trouble already. You know the law about homosexual activity. It's illegal unless it's between consenting adults and you're well under age. There's also the question of Garston being on the run from the police . . .'

'I didn't know that!' the boy cried in desperate protest.

'. . . which could earn you quite a long Borstal sentence. So be sensible. Let's have the truth about Garston.'

'I've told it already. He didn't go out either evening except down the fish-and-chip shop.'

Flinging back his chair so violently that it nearly fell over, Nunn gathered up his papers and made for the door. Finch, rising more slowly, saw the whole of the boy's face quiver as if every nerve in it jumped simultaneously and his eyes swim with tears, but the mouth was set in a sullen line even though the bottom lip trembled like a child's.

Outside, Nunn said more moderately, 'Poor little sod. I suppose we'd better wheel in the social services and try to get him sorted out although, in his case, it's probably too late; the damage has already been done. You know, Jack, I reckon our generation has a lot to answer for.'

'You think it's our fault?' Finch asked.

'Well, someone should have told him the difference between what's real and what isn't. Instead of which, he comes looking for a dream and finds Garston, for Christ's sake. All the same, he's lying.'

'You're sure?' Finch himself wasn't convinced.

'He's got to be,' Nunn retorted. 'Garston did those murders. They've got his stamp all over them.'

'But supposing Bentley isn't lying?' Finch put in.

Nunn gave him a sharp, sideways look.

'Then you've opened an entirely new can of worms.' He sounded dismissive. After all, it wasn't his problem.

'There's this other boyfriend of Chivers, the one Garston mentioned,' Finch pointed out.

'Garston could have been making it up,'

'I don't think so.'

'Neither do I,' Nunn admitted. 'He didn't even know he'd been tricked into admitting it. Mind you, if Garston's on the level and Ray's boyfriend is, as he said, someone high up in the Civil Service, it'd give him a motive for wanting Ray dead.'

'Blackmail?' Finch suggested. 'It'd crossed my mind, too.'

'God knows how you'll find him, though,' Nunn remarked not unsympathetically. 'At least with criminals like Garston we know where to look for their rat-runs. You can't start turning over Surbiton or Chorley Wood hunting for an unknown killer. Any leads?'

'Nothing yet,' Finch admitted.

'Then the best of British, Jack. Let me know how it goes and if there's anything I can do to help. I'm pushing off now. I've got to get Garston and Bentley back to London. By the way, I've arranged transport for you. PC Watts will run you back to Chelmsford. He's waiting outside.'

They walked together to the door of the station. It was still only eight o'clock and the little town was hardly awake yet, the shops still closed although the first local commuters, heading for the offices of Clacton, were already queueing at the bus-stop.

As Finch walked down the steps towards the waiting car, he looked back but Nunn, as impatient as ever, hadn't waited and all Finch saw was a back view of him retreating hurriedly, eager to get on with the job. For him, at least, the morning had been highly successful. Finch could only hope that the same success would come his way before too long.

II

But luck seemed to elude him for over the next four days nothing happened. There was plenty of activity – people arrived to make statements, reports were submitted, Finch laboriously typed out his own, but all of it was mere written confirmation of what he knew already from the verbal accounts. Not one new fact or piece of evidence was added and, as the files of reports gradually thickened, he began to think despondently that the investigation had been reduced to nothing but paper.

He hadn't seen Marion Greave either. She had called at headquarters on Monday afternoon when he happened to be out and, in his absence, had left her own report, neatly typewritten and enclosed, together with the photographs and drawings, in a strong manila envelope. She, at least, had added a few new facts or, rather, had substantiated what Finch had already guessed: the times of death of the two victims. In Ray Chivers' case she had not been able to fix the time too precisely, stating that it had occurred between eleven o'clock on Friday evening and four a.m. on Saturday. In the Aspinell case, she was able to be more definite, the contents of the dead man's stomach allowing her to establish the time of death at approximately six a.m. on Sunday. The wound, she added, was identical to the fracture in Chivers' skull which also confirmed Finch's assumption that both victims had been murdered with the same weapon.

So Aspinell had died at just about dawn, Finch thought,

remembering the grey light which had broken over the caravan site on his own early morning excursion with Nunn: late enough not to arouse too much suspicion on Aspinell's part but too early, especially on a Sunday morning, for anyone to be up and about in the streets.

It seemed just his luck to have missed seeing her and, on his return to the office, he rang her number only to hear her recorded voice announce that she was out of the surgery on house visits and would he please leave a message together with his name, address and telephone number when he heard the tone?

He hung up without speaking.

On the same afternoon, he also received Marsh's reports on the fingerprints found at the two scenes of crime but they, too, added little in the way of new evidence. In the Charlton Road house, Stanley Aspinell's were found and two other sets which, on sending an officer to the Southalls' home to fingerprint Martin Southall and his wife, were identified as belonging to them. No other prints were found, which suggested the murderer had been careful not to touch anything.

Several sets had also been found in Holly Lodge, apart from Ray Chivers', some of them so worn and rubbed that Finch suspected they belonged to the previous occupants who, he supposed wearily, could be traced and their prints checked if necessary. The report also confirmed the fact that several surfaces had been wiped clean, almost certainly deliberately.

But the last paragraph contained one piece of information which was worth having. In the living-room at Holly Lodge a quite separate set of prints, not Chivers', had been picked up on the furniture, photographs of which had been included with Marsh's report.

And they weren't Frank Garston's either, as Finch discovered when he compared them to those which had been sent down from Scotland Yard after Garston's arrest. It was another piece of negative evidence like so much else in the investigation, not proving conclusively that Garston hadn't murdered Ray Chivers. After all, he could have been careful not to leave any evidence behind him which would have proved his presence at either murder scene, as the lack of prints at Aspinell's house tended to suggest. But at least it provided Finch with the evidence that someone else other than Garston had been present in the downstairs living-room at Holly Lodge, possibly the murderer if he believed, as he was inclined to do, Garston's alibi.

He would send the prints off, of course, to the Yard to be checked against their records but, unless they were on file, it would be a waste of time, Finch thought gloomily.

From what Nunn had told him, Benny Costello didn't have a police record and as it was unlikely that the other suspect, Ray Chivers' new boyfriend whom Garston had mentioned, had broken the law, there was no way of knowing if the prints belonged to either of them until both men could be picked up.

Finch spread the two sets of photographs, Marion Greave's and Marsh's, out on his desk. It wasn't much from which to build up an Identikit picture of a killer – a set of fingerprints and some close-up shots of a wound in a dead man's skull but, in the absence of anything else, it was all he had to go on.

It was a point he made to Boyce and Munro when they returned later that day from their inquiries at the furniture shops in Chelmsford. Finch could tell by their faces as they came tramping into his office that these results, too, were negative.

'Nix,' Boyce said succinctly, lowering himself into a chair. He looked pinched by the cold and his hacking cough had returned.

'Right!' Finch snapped. 'Then tomorrow you switch the inquiries to London.'

'Oh, God!' Boyce muttered under his breath.

'I found out something that could be useful,' Munro put in. 'One shopkeeper was able to tell me a bit about the stuff. It's imported from France and is on the pricey side. That's why he didn't stock it. I got the name of the import firm from him. If we contact them, they could probably give us a list of retailers who bought the furniture from them, which would narrow the search down.'

'Good for you, Colin,' Finch said approvingly, ignoring

Boyce who chose that moment to blow his nose loudly, forcing Munro to raise his voice. 'I'll leave you to check that out. Once you've got a list of London retailers, you and Tom can work out individual schedules for each man. Start from the West End stores like Selfridges and fan out from there.'

'Very good, sir,' Munro said promptly.

Finch looked across at Boyce who was now making a great play of putting away his handkerchief.

'You heard that, Tom?' he asked sharply.

Boyce looked up, his expression sulky, like a schoolkid's suddenly called to order, Finch thought with exasperation.

'Yes, I did. Sir.'

The last word was added almost as an afterthought.

Finch hid his anger as he motioned the two men closer to the desk to inspect the photographs while he gave them a brief résumé of their potential importance.

When he had finished, Munro asked, 'Dr Greave made the drawings?' with an astonished approval as if he would not have expected a woman to show so much intelligence or professional skill. To his surprise, Finch reacted as he imagined Marion Greave might have done. Hearing the remark as if with her ears, he realized what it must be like for a woman in her position to encounter such an example of male prejudice. It was an uncomfortable experience and also a humbling one. He, too, had been guilty of showing much the same attitude on occasions.

'Any ideas on the type of weapon used?' he asked abruptly.

'Like a baseball bat, you said?' Boyce asked.

'Only smaller.'

'Could it have been a kid-sized bat?'

'It's possible. I don't know if they're manufactured. You can check on that for me, Tom.'

Boyce fell silent as if regretting having spoken.

Munro said, 'I've had a bit of experience of these East End crooks. Some of them will go to a lot of trouble to have a cosh made up. A sort of professional pride, if you like. There used to be an ex-con in Bermondsey who turned them out. He learnt how to work a lathe in the prison workshop – fancied himself as something of an expert.'

144

He spoke with that slightly assertive air of his as if eager to demonstrate a more extensive knowledge than Boyce, and Finch looked covertly at the other Sergeant, noting his reaction. As he had suspected, Boyce's face had taken on a closed, sullen expression which exasperated the Chief Inspector. Although he could sympathize to some extent with Boyce's attitude, he nevertheless felt that the Sergeant should, as a professional policeman, appreciate the specialized knowledge which the younger man was bringing to the case.

'Is he still around?' he asked, wondering if it might be a possible lead.

Munro shook his head.

'No, he died about five years ago. His clients gave him one of those big East End funerals. There were wreaths galore: empty chairs and pearly gates made out of chrysanths and an all-night knees-up afterwards.'

'Well, if you get any ideas, let me know,' Finch said. As the two men turned towards the door, he added, 'I'd like a word with you, Tom.'

The time had come to speak, he felt. He had put it off for long enough. It was a spur of the moment decision and he had no idea what the hell he was going to say.

As soon as the door closed behind Munro, Finch resumed his seat behind the desk, motioning Boyce to sit down also. Judging by his expression, the Sergeant realized that this was going to be no friendly tête-à-tête. The positioning of them both, separated by the width of the desk top, suggested a formal interview.

'Look, Tom,' Finch began, 'I don't want to pull rank on you. God knows you and I know each other too well for that. But I can't let the situation between you and Munro go on any longer. I realize he can be a bit of a know-all at times, but all the same he's a damned good officer and we're lucky to have him in the team. Tomorrow, you're going to have to work fairly closely with him, organizing the inquiries in London, and I'm not having you or anybody else making a balls-up of the investigation because you and Munro don't happen to see eye to eye. Is that clear?'

During this speech, Boyce did not once attempt to look the

Chief Inspector in the face but remained gazing down at his hands which were clasped round each knee as if holding them in place.

He didn't even look up as he said, 'Yes, sir,' in a subdued voice in answer to Finch's final question. Finch found himself half-wishing that the Sergeant had lost his temper or protested, at least had shown some more positive reaction. Putting him in his place had been almost too easy and it aroused in Finch an unexpected and quite irrational sense of guilt as if he, not Boyce, were in the wrong.

'I shan't refer to it again,' Finch added. It was on the tip of his tongue to apologize but he resisted the temptation.

'Is that all, sir?' Boyce asked, still looking down at his hands.

'Yes, Tom; that's all.'

He watched as Boyce got to his feet and walked heavily out of the room. His back view, particularly his neck, expressed a complexity of emotions: pathos, dejection and also an aggrieved self-consciousness as if Boyce himself were aware of the figure he was cutting as the door closed behind him.

'Oh, Christ!' Finch said out loud and slammed the Chivers' file down on his desk.

Any further work was impossible. Thanks to Boyce, he wasn't in the mood and, after fidgeting about the office for ten minutes, he sat down again at the desk and reached for the telephone. There was no point in sitting about doing nothing. To take his mind off Boyce, he'd try ringing Marion Greave again. It seemed an evening for sudden decisions and he felt the need to do something different, incautious even. But half-way through dialling her number, he changed his mind again.

Why not call at her house? he asked himself. He could then thank her in person for sending the report and the photographs. And if he needed an excuse for the visit, he could think up some detail which he wanted to discuss with her. The time of Ray Chivers' death would do. He could ask if there were any chances of it being fixed more precisely. At the same time, he could ask her out to dinner. A new Greek restaurant had opened in town and he could say he was on his way there and would she like to come with him? Not that he cared much for foreign food, but he suspected she might.

The plan seemed foolproof and without giving himself the chance to change his mind again, he rang his sister to tell her he wouldn't be home for dinner that evening.

She sounded disappointed.

'But, Jack, there's a chicken casserole in the oven.'

'Won't it keep till tomorrow? Only I'm up to my eyes in work.'

He was ashamed at the ease with which the lie rose to his lips and felt even more culpable when she asked, her voice full of concern, 'You will make sure you have something to eat?'

'Oh, I'll grab a sandwich,' he replied and hung up quickly before she could say anything more, feeling he was betraying her.

God knows how much he owed her. She had looked after him for so many years. At the very least, he ought to have been frank with her. But what the hell could he say? There's this woman I'm attracted to?

Hardly.

Such an admission he knew would damage their relationship, a risk he wasn't prepared to make until he knew how far he was committed for, after all, it involved no more, for the time being, than a dinner date.

Now that the die was cast, he felt almost jaunty.

Thank God, he thought, as he shaved quickly in the men's cloakroom, that he had put on a clean shirt that morning. His suit had seen better days though and he made up his mind that it was about time he bought a new one, even though he hated the fuss which buying clothes always entailed and the ridiculous decisions he was forced into making such as how many buttons and did he want one or two vents in the back of the jacket?

Examining his cheeks and chin in the mirror above the basin, he met his own eyes and grinned sheepishly at his reflection.

He was going on a date! Him, after all these years! And the absurd part was that he felt like a sixteen-year-old again on his way to a Youth Club dance in the village hall where a girl, whose

147

name he had now forgotten although he could remember her blue eyes and plump little hands, might smile at him when he went up to claim her in the Excuse Me foxtrot.

He kept his speed down deliberately as he drove to Marion Greave's house – God knows why. Even he wasn't sure. It was partly to extend the sense of anticipation perhaps and partly out of a lingering sense of guilt towards his sister and Boyce which he felt might be assuaged if he didn't rush off too eagerly in pursuit of his own pleasure.

Turning into her road which was dimly lit, he counted the gates. Four on the right and the next was hers. As he parked the car and got out, he noticed that there were no lights on in the house apart from one in the hall which he could see shining through the reeded glass panels in the door. The surgery, too, was in darkness. But the idea that she might be out did not cross his mind. He was so utterly confident that she would be there and that she would invite him again into that jewelled room with its flowers and pictures and that later they would sit facing each other across a dining-table. He had the report and photographs in his pockets. The words he would say to her when she opened the door were already rehearsed in his mind.

It was only after he had knocked three times and no one had answered that he admitted to himself she might be out.

It was ridiculous to feel so rejected. After all, she hadn't known he was coming. All the same he felt as dismissed as if she had slammed the door in his face.

Walking away, his shoulders hunched, he was conscious that he was walking in much the same manner as Boyce had done when he had left the room, the same lowered head, exposing the nape of his neck, a similar sense of being too aware of the angle of his spine.

It was pathetic! he thought angrily, slamming the car door shut. Well, that would teach him a lesson. It was the last time he'd go rushing off on the spur of the moment in the hope of seeing her.

Starting the engine and turning the car in the road, it suddenly occurred to him that he had nowhere arranged to eat that evening. He could always go home, of course. Dorothy would welcome him, delighted that the chicken casserole would not have to be served up reheated the following night. But to do so seemed like an admission of defeat.

In the end, he had a sandwich after all, a ham one and not very fresh either, left over, he suspected, from the lunch-time trade and served by a middle-aged, worn-looking barmaid in a dreary little back-street public house.

As he chewed his way through it alone at a corner table and drank a pint of bitter he had ordered to go with it, he took the photographs from his pocket and studied them again, more for the sake of something to do than because he needed reminding of their contents.

But as he looked at them and reconsidered the type of weapon that might have caused the wound in Ray Chivers' skull, turning over in his mind Marion Greave's description of its shape, like a small baseball bat, a comparison with something else flickered briefly at the back of his consciousness. It was connected, too, with what Nunn had told him about Garston's impersonation of a police sergeant in order to gain entry to Mitchell's house in Hampstead although for a moment he could not link the two ideas.

'Finished?'

It was the barmaid doing a round of the tables to collect up dirty glasses and, as Finch nodded, she whisked away his empty plate and glass. At the same time, he hurriedly thrust the prints into his pocket. They were not the type of close-up shots he wanted to be seen studying in public.

After she had gone, he re-examined them but the idea – if it was as definite as that, rather a mere impression, a half-formed notion – had totally vanished and no amount of poring over the photographs would bring it back.

It would return though; he felt quite confident of that. It had happened before. At some point during the next few days, something else would happen to jog his memory, a stray remark, a casual observation, and the connection would be re-established.

In a better mood, he buttoned up his raincoat and made for the door, where it suddenly occurred to him that for the past three quarters of an hour he hadn't once thought of Marion Greave. The realization pleased him and turning back he called out cheerfully, 'Goodnight!'

The barmaid's haggard face looked at him in surprise. For a moment, she seemed on the point of ignoring him. Then, smiling, she called back, 'Goodnight, dear!'

12

But his confidence seemed to be misplaced for, although he re-examined the photographs several times over the next few days, the idea remained elusive and refused to be inveigled into full consciousness. He even made little drawings of a baseball bat on a sheet of paper but they evoked no other image than that of a badly-drawn object like the upper part of a fat exclamation mark and, in disgust, he crumpled them up and flung them into the waste-paper basket.

The inquiries in London regarding the furniture were proving as fruitless. Munro had obtained a list of retailers from the importer, over a hundred in all, and Finch had assigned five men to the inquiries, all he could spare.

God knows what was happening between Munro and Boyce. Finch assumed they had got together and amicably drawn up a schedule, but he only saw them in the evenings when they reported back after the day's inquiries, short interview sessions at which both men looked tired, although Munro seemed to be standing up to the strain better than Boyce. But then he was a younger man.

Finch sympathized with them both. From his own experience, he knew there was nothing more disheartening than tramping about in the cold from one address to the other, asking questions to which the answer was always a negative.

On the second evening, he tried a direct approach to Boyce.

'Are you all right?' he asked.

But Boyce chose to reply as if the question referred merely to his physical health.

'Bloody tired,' he said gloomily. 'And I think I've caught another cold.'

He certainly looked far from well but the response, so depressingly typical of the Sergeant in one of his low states of mind, failed to evoke any answering guilt in Finch. He had passed through that stage of his relationship with Boyce and could now regard him with only a distanced compassion.

'You want to treat yourself to a bottle of whisky for a few night-caps,' he suggested.

'I have,' Boyce replied and there the conversation ended.

As for himself, Finch remained in his office, on hand in case one of the men telephoned in to report finding the shop where the furniture had been bought. In the meantime, he got on with the paper-work, checking through the reports and writing up his own. It was a task he normally disliked doing, but the sight of the weather outside the window, a constant fine grey drizzle, made the job tolerable. At least he was indoors in the warm and dry.

While he was dealing with the paper-work, he also wrote a short letter to Marion Greave, friendly but not too personal, thanking her for sending the photographs and the reports.

When he had done that, the letter looked too brief and he added another paragraph asking her if it were possible to establish more precisely the time of Ray Chivers' death, the same reason he had thought up as an excuse for calling on her. The answer would probably be a negative, he concluded as he stuck down the flap of the envelope, but the information would be useful if she could supply it.

As he put it in his out-tray with the other official correspondence, he thought, Well, that's that. Unless something else cropped up on which he needed her professional assistance, that relationship, like his and Boyce's, would become distanced although he might take up his promise to take her out to dinner one evening. They would meet, however, on an impersonal basis, he decided, two people of shared professional interest talking shop over a meal.

His moment of madness had passed. He was a middle-aged police Inspector again, not a schoolboy excited over the prospect of a date.

Her telephone call the following day took him by surprise. Expecting it was from one of the men on the London inquiries, he picked up the receiver eagerly; the case was on the move again. For a moment, he didn't even recognize her voice at the end of the line.

'I got your letter this morning,' she said. 'About Chivers' death, I can't fix the timing accurately but I can tell you this. He'd been drinking about an hour before he died – spirits, not beer. If you can establish exactly when he had his last drink, I could then work out more precisely when he died.'

It wasn't a lot of help. Chivers might have had his last drink at six o'clock when the pubs opened or eleven o'clock when they closed. There was no way of telling, although it might be worthwhile checking on the pubs to find out which one he'd been to, Finch thought. It wasn't the one on the corner, the Carpenters' Arms. That had been checked out already; Chivers hadn't been drinking there on the Friday night. And as there were no bottles of spirit found at the house, only empty tins of lager, it seemed likely that he had gone out to drink. Unless, of course, the murderer had brought a bottle with him and had taken the evidence away with him afterwards.

With these thoughts running through his head, he gave only scant consideration to his answer.

'Thanks. That could be useful. By the way, I called at your house on Monday evening but you were out.'

As soon as the words were out of his mouth, he regretted them. God knows what prompted him to make the remark. There was no need for her to know and he half-expected her response would be a surprised silence.

Instead, she replied, 'I'm sorry I missed you. I was having dinner with friends that evening. It's my night off. The surgery's closed on Mondays.'

He was stupid not to have checked the board at the gate on which her surgery hours were displayed, he thought.

At the same time, the genuine regret in her voice at having

missed seeing him plunged him once again into the old uncertainty.

But was it genuine or was she being merely politely pleasant? It was difficult to tell over the telephone when he had only her voice to judge by. And who were the people she was dining with? Although the word suggested more than one person, she might have had her own escort, some man who had taken her there and driven her home afterwards.

He heard himself mumbling, 'I was just passing so I thought I'd call.'

Which only made the matter worse, for not only did it belittle his visit but, as an excuse, it hardly stood up to examination. She lived in a cul-de-sac. There was no possible way that he could have driven past her house except with the intention of calling on her.

The same thought might have been in her mind for she said with a note of amusement in her voice, 'Then do call again next time you're passing and I'll give you coffee.'

He hung up, feeling angry with himself and frustrated by the whole damned stupid business. He was back to where he had been the first time he had met her and the decision he had just made about keeping their relationship impersonal had already gone out of the window.

For the rest of the day he was in a bad mood. Word was passed round headquarters so that anyone who approached him did so cautiously, their careful, formal voices and expressions adding to his sense of moody isolation.

Munro's call two days later lifted his spirits. It came at four o'clock on Friday afternoon just when he was thinking that it seemed the inquiries would extend into the following week.

'I've traced the furniture, sir!' Munro's voice sounded excited. 'Luckily the man who bought it paid by cheque and the manager asked him to write his address on the back. He then made a note of it in the sales' book. It's a small shop, just off Baker Street and they like to keep a record of customers' names and addresses so they can let them know when they're having any special promotions.'

'The manager's sure it's the same furniture?' Finch asked. The news seemed too good to be true.

'Oh, yes, sir, positive. Remember those small labels stuck underneath the frames? Well, that's the shop's system of recording merchandise. The number is entered in the sales' book along with the customer's name and address.'

'And what are they?' Finch asked, his pen poised over his notebook.

'The name's Hugo Bannister and the address is . . .'

The rest of the sentence was lost in a metallic clanging noise in the background.

'Can you repeat that?' Finch demanded.

'Sorry, sir. I'm phoning from the shop and something's just been delivered. The address is: Flat 1c, Grantham House, Maddox Road. That's not far from the shop.'

'I'll look it up in the A–Z street directory,' Finch told him. 'Now, look, Munro, I don't want you to do anything until I get there. Do you understand? Don't attempt to approach this man or where he lives. I'll leave a message here for Boyce so that the address can be passed on to him when he phones in. I'll meet you both there between half past five and six, depending on the traffic. And don't make yourself look conspicuous by hanging about outside Bannister's address. Go and get yourself tea in the meantime or look round Madame Tussaud's.'

'Will do,' Munro replied and hung up.

In fact, it was nearly a quarter past six before Finch arrived at the address and found somewhere to park. The rush hour had begun and he was stuck in Marylebone Road for nearly twenty minutes, cursing under his breath as he inched his way forwards.

As he turned into Maddox Road and parked the car, he saw Boyce, a few parking meters further on, get out of his car while Munro, strolling along casually on the opposite side of the street, crossed over towards them.

As he walked forward to meet them, Finch glanced about him. It was a short, residential road of large houses and the older type of mansion flats, solidly built in red brick with steps up to the front doors and deep basements separated from the pavement by railings. They looked discreetly prosperous in a substantial Edwardian style with their sash windows and heavy front doors, suggesting a lost era of port and roast pheasant, gentlemen's clubs and buttoned leather armchairs.

Grantham House was one of the mansion blocks and, as he walked past it, Finch glanced up the steps at the front door with its coloured glass panels and the rows of brass bell-pushes beside it.

They conferred briefly on the pavement a few doors away.

'It's not going to take three of us to interview Hugo Bannister,' Finch said. 'If he's what I think he is, Ray Chivers' boyfriend, then we've got to tread carefully. Garston said he was high-up in the Civil Service and, judging by that,' indicating with a backward jerk of his head the reserved, dignified façade of Grantham House, 'he's right. You don't find a desk clerk living in a place like that.'

It was on the tip of his tongue to choose Munro. After all, he had discovered the name and address and it seemed only right to pick him out to see the job finished. But some lingering residue of guilt towards Boyce made the Chief Inspector change his mind. There was a more practical reason, too. He and Boyce had worked together so often in the past that they had developed an effective interviewing technique, an advantage which Finch was loath to relinquish.

'You come with me, Tom,' he said. Turning to Munro, he added, 'You've done your bit, Colin, and I'm grateful. You can push off home now.'

He was a little surprised at Munro's lack of response. Many men, finding themselves passed over in favour of someone else, would have shown at least disappointment. Munro must have had his feelings well under control, for all he said was, 'Very good, sir,' before nodding to Boyce, as if conceding the victory to him, and walking away to his car.

In comparison, Boyce made no effort to hide his reaction. Grinning perkily, as much delighted, Finch suspected, at Munro's defeat as at his own success, he stepped out jauntily at Finch's side as they returned the few yards to Grantham House.

At the top of the steps, Finch paused to study the names

beside the bell-pushes. Hugo Bannister occupied a first-floor apartment and, glancing up, he saw the front windows on that floor were lit up. But as there was no way of knowing whether they were Bannister's or not, Finch rang the bell marked 'Porter'.

The door was opened by an elderly man in a dark red uniform with brass buttons and what looked like small crests on the collar-tabs. A faint aroma of whisky hung about him, only partly disguised by the smell of peppermint.

'I'm making a few official inquiries,' Finch announced, producing his identification at which the man peered before showing them into a large, square entrance hall, floored with yellow and brown tiles set in a vaguely Moorish pattern and lined with dark panelling. It was like walking into a huge cigar box, rich and dimly lit, with a faint, spicy scent about it. On the left, a staircase with a mahogany rail, its dark red carpeting held in place by brass rods, led to the upper floors while a porter's cubicle had been built in to the space beneath it. Facing them was a small, gilt lift looking like an old-fashioned bird-cage.

'I believe Mr Hugo Bannister is one of your residents?' Finch continued.

'That's right,' the porter replied. 'You want to see him? He's at home; got in about a quarter of an hour ago.' His little blue eyes were lively with curiosity. 'Do you want me to phone him and tell him you're on your way up to see him?'

'No,' Finch said sharply, 'we'll announce ourselves.'

As they walked towards the stairs, the man called after them, 'He's on the first floor. You can take the lift.'

'We'll walk up,' Finch replied over his shoulder.

He didn't bother to add that it would probably be quicker. The lift looked a slow-moving noisy contraption and he didn't want his arrival heralded by the clash of its gates as they emerged on the landing outside Hugo Bannister's flat.

The stairs ascended to a long landing off which three doors opened. 1c was at the far end and would face the back of the building, Finch guessed.

'Ready?' he said to Boyce, his finger over the bell.

Boyce nodded. He had assumed his solemn, on-duty, interviewing expression, all traces of his earlier jubilation at Munro's discomfiture expunged.

Finch pressed the button.

The door was opened by a tall, lean, distinguished looking man in his late forties or early fifties, with thinning dark hair which had receded to reveal a high, bony forehead. His features wore a fastidious expression as if their presence outside his apartment offended him.

'Mr Bannister?' Finch asked pleasantly.

Hugo Bannister examined the two men with quick suspicion. Since Benny's unexpected arrival at the cottage, he regarded all visitors with mistrust. Besides, it was rare for anyone to call, especially strangers. The two men, however, didn't have the appearance of being friends of either Ray or Benny. The man who had addressed him was of short, stocky build, dressed in a shabby raincoat and with the broad, fresh face of a countryman. His companion was tall and bulky and wore a self-consciously formal expression as if he had deliberately arranged his features to convey a serious purpose behind the visit.

It was this expression which warned Hugo of their identity.

'You're from the police,' he said.

'Detective Chief Inspector Finch from Chelmsford CID and Detective Sergeant Boyce,' Finch replied. He had produced his identification but Hugo Bannister hardly glanced at it.

'You'd better come in,' he said and showed them into a hall and from there into the drawing-room.

As they entered, Finch looked about him with rapid, covert glances. In some ways, it reminded him of Marion Greave's drawing-room. Like hers, it was full of books and the windows looked out on to trees; plane trees this time, in a small courtyard behind the building. But in every other respect how different! Her room had radiated colour and comfort. This was formally beautiful as if everything in it had been chosen to represent a certain life-style and not from personal taste.

He wondered what Ray Chivers, with his East End background of pubs and drinking clubs, had thought of this setting with its crystal light fittings and elaborately swagged, heavy velvet curtains.

Hugo Bannister indicated two small armchairs with carved arms and satin covers – probably antique and valuable, Finch thought as he lowered himself into his, but nowhere near as comfortable as Marion Greave's. These did not invite relaxation nor the tête-à-tête approach with which he preferred to conduct an interview. It was impossible to be anything but formal in such a chair.

Not that Hugo Bannister's demeanour suggested he would welcome informality. He had crossed the room to pour himself a whisky and his narrow back, bent over the glasses on the side-table, looked forbiddingly severe.

'Will you join me?' he asked and, when Finch refused, he added, 'No, I suppose you can't. You're on duty.'

It was a statement rather than a question and Finch acknowledged the truth of it with a small inclination of the head.

With his back turned as he poured his drink, Hugo Bannister came to a decision. It would be pointless, he realized, to attempt to deny his relationship with Ray or his knowledge of Ray's death. These men were from Chelmsford CID. That fact alone suggested that they were conducting an investigation into Ray's murder.

God knows how they'd discovered his address, but now that they were here he almost welcomed their presence. It was all over: the doubt, the uncertainty, the fear.

He could make a clean breast of it and he smiled wryly at the phrase which reminded him of his prep school. Its motto had been Veritas Honore – Truth with Honour. Well, he didn't suppose much honour would emerge from this particular situation, but the truth would have to be told nevertheless, no matter what the consequences. It would finish his career, of course. He worked in too sensitive an area of government for him to survive the scandal. Resignation would be the cleanest way out.

'You've come about Ray Chivers,' he announced.

He had taken up a position standing by the fireplace, holding his glass, although he did not attempt to drink from it.

Perched on his chair, Finch had to look up at the man's face which still bore that look of fastidious distaste.

'You knew him,' Finch replied. His remark also was a statement, not a question.

'Yes. I met him about six months ago. We were lovers on a casual basis. There were no commitments.' Remembering Benny's words, his voice was bleak. 'I also knew he was murdered.' Almost as an afterthought, he added, 'I didn't kill him, however. I was told of his murder by a friend of his who discovered the body.'

'His name?' Finch asked.

Opposite him, Boyce took out his pen and notebook and Finch saw Hugo Bannister glance across at him with an expression of amused disdain as if the Sergeant's action had touched in him some wry quirk of humour.

'I only knew him as Benny. As for his address, he's staying at my cottage in Suffolk. He arrived there last weekend. The address is Thatch End, Lambourne. It's not far from Flatford.'

He paused to give Boyce time to write this down before continuing, 'He also denied murdering Ray but I suppose I shall be suspected of sheltering him. What's the correct term?'

'Assisting an offender,' Finch replied.

Despite Hugo Bannister's coldness, he felt a grudging admiration for the man. There was a dry, unemotional judiciousness about him which the Chief Inspector recognized and respected as a form of courage. It would be degrading to both of them not to make the gravity of his position exactly clear to him.

'You realize,' Finch continued, 'that the same charge could be brought against you with regard to Ray Chivers? He was on the run from the police.'

'Yes, Benny told me that, too, although I had no idea at the time. Ray said he was in trouble with an East End gang. That's why I helped him.' Raising his narrow shoulders in a self-deprecatory gesture, he added, 'I'm afraid this must sound to you like a series of rather weak excuses for which I apologize.'

Finch made no direct response. Instead, he asked, 'I'd like a statement of your movements last Friday night.'

'I called on Ray at the house in Chelmsford.'

'At what time?' Boyce asked, raising his head.

'At about half past seven, I think. I was driving down to

spend the weekend in Suffolk and, as Chelmsford is on the route, I stopped at the house and took Ray out for a drink.'

'What did he have?' Finch asked, remembering Marion Greave's comment about the spirit found in Chivers' stomach.

Hugo Bannister raised his eyebrows briefly at this seemingly trivial question.

'He had a rum and coke. Two, in fact,' he replied. 'I can't remember the name of the public house although, if it's important, I could no doubt find it again. We left at roughly half past ten when I drove Ray back to Holly Lodge. He was expecting Benny to call that evening. He'd left a note for him in the letter-box and, as I returned, I saw a man, whom I later recognized as Benny, waiting for him at the front door.'

'Did you go into the house?' Finch asked.

'No. It was already late and I still had to drive to Suffolk. I might add that Ray had told me Benny was his brother although, as soon as I saw him, I doubted this fact.'

His tone was unemotional, simply stating the facts, and there was no indication either in his voice or his expression that, as he spoke, he was recalling with painful clarity his last glimpse of Ray as he passed through the dazzle of the headlights.

'I then drove to the cottage,' he continued.

'Just a moment,' Finch interrupted. 'Let's go back to the point where you dropped Ray off at Holly Lodge. Did you happen to see anybody in the street, a passer-by?'

Hugo Bannister looked annoyed at the interruption.

'No, I didn't.'

'An elderly man with a dog?'

'I've already told you, Chief Inspector, I saw nobody.'

It was Boyce's turn to ask a question.

'What sort of car do you own, Mr Bannister?'

'A Rover.'

'And its colour?'

'Black, but I don't see the point of the question.'

Finch knew what was in the Sergeant's mind, however. Martin Southall, Stanley Aspinell's son-in-law, had said that his father-in-law had seemed uncharacteristically interested in cars and had asked specifically about the possible make of a large, dark vehicle.

'Go on,' he said, addressing Bannister. 'You drove to Suffolk. What time did you arrive?'

'I'm not sure. About a quarter to twelve, I think.'

'Any witnesses?'

Hugo Bannister gave a faint smile.

'No. I live alone both here and at the cottage – at least, I usually do.'

'And Saturday? What did you do that evening?'

'I was alone in the cottage until Benny arrived. He told me he had learnt of the address from Ray and he simply turned up at about eight o'clock, looking for somewhere to hide. He was frightened Ray's murderer might be looking for him.'

'Did he mention a name?'

'Yes, he did. It was Garston, I believe. He'd been with Ray on a burglary in Hampstead at which a policeman was killed. Benny was convinced that Garston had murdered Ray and would kill him too.'

Finch heard Boyce shift his position in his chair but refrained from looking at him. His own expression was bland as he asked, 'You believed him?'

Again the narrow shoulders lifted in that disdainful gesture.

'It seemed plausible.'

'So you did nothing?'

'I considered telephoning the police. I even drove to the telephone box in the village but I didn't put through the call.'

Although Finch could guess the answer, he nevertheless pressed the question. It would be interesting, he thought, to discover just how far Hugo Bannister's impassivity would extend.

'Why not?'

Hugo Bannister looked directly at him.

'I was anxious about my reputation if the truth came out, Chief Inspector,' he replied.

Top marks for honesty and courage, Finch thought.

'And so you allowed Benny to stay?'

'Yes.'

'Which room did he occupy?'

It seemed an impertinent question, but it had to be asked.

'The spare bedroom.'

'So he could have left the cottage during the night without your knowledge?'

'It's possible but unlikely. I'm a light sleeper and would have heard him. I don't know whether Benny sleeps heavily or not so, as far as I am concerned, he may not be able to vouch for my movements.' He seemed suddenly aware of the significance of the questions because he added, 'But why Saturday night? According to Benny, Ray must have been murdered on Friday. At least, Benny told me he'd found Ray dead on Saturday morning.'

His perplexity seemed genuine and Finch was inclined to believe that Bannister knew nothing of Stanley Aspinell's murder – unless, of course, the man was a damned good actor.

Side-stepping the question, he asked, 'Did Benny say anything about finding some money hidden at Holly Lodge?'

As he had intended, his question diverted Hugo Bannister's attention from his own.

'Yes, as a matter of fact, he did. I forgot to mention it. He said Ray must have had several thousand pounds from the Hampstead burglary but it was missing. He assumed Garston had taken it when he murdered Ray.'

Finch looked across at Boyce inquiringly, inviting him to ask any questions he wanted but Boyce gave a slight shake of his head and the two men rose to their feet. The interview was over for the time being. A more searching cross-examination would take place when they took down a final, written statement.

Hugo Bannister put down his untasted glass of whisky on the mantelpiece.

'I suppose you'll want me to come with you?' he asked.

'Yes, sir.' It was Boyce who replied. Finch usually left it to him to complete the formalities. 'You'll be taken to police headquarters in Chelmsford and asked to make a complete statement.'

'And shall I be charged?' Hugo Bannister inquired, his voice expressionless.

Boyce also side-stepped the question.

'You may be held, sir, pending further inquiries.'

'I should bring an overcoat with you, if I were you,' Finch added, not unkindly. 'It's quite cold outside. My Sergeant will come with you while you fetch it.'

Hugo Bannister smiled bleakly.

'If you insist, Chief Inspector, although I assure you I have no intention of either attempting to escape or committing suicide.'

As he walked to the door, Finch said *sotto voce* to Boyce, 'I'll have to warn headquarters we're coming; put in a report. I'll ring from downstairs. There should be a phone in the porter's lodge.'

It was better, he decided, than using the telephone in Bannister's flat. He might be asked for details and, in view of Bannister's own fastidious reticence, Finch was reluctant to run the risk of being overheard discussing the man's involvement in the case.

Boyce nodded and left the room, Finch following behind him into the hall where he let himself out of the flat by the front door.

The porter's cubicle was empty although, as he reached the bottom of the stairs, a door set in the panelling beside it, which he assumed led down into the basement, opened and the porter emerged, smelling even more strongly of peppermint and hurriedly buttoning his uniform coat.

Finch suspected that whenever he had the chance, the man retreated downstairs to his own quarters to console himself with a bottle of whisky. To give the man his due, the job, which seemed to entail nothing more strenuous than taking in mail for delivery to the individual apartments and watching over the comings and goings of the tenants, must have had its tedious moments which he relieved by a little quiet illicit drinking.

'I'd like to use your phone,' Finch told him.

'Help yourself,' the porter said, opening the cubicle door for him. 'But you'll have to pay. I have to log every call that goes out on that line. It's management policy.'

Finch nodded and shut the door.

The cubicle was tiny and was fitted with a glazed hatch which could be opened up to allow the porter to speak to callers. To the left of it was a bench-top on which the telephone receiver was standing and above that was a rack of pigeon-holes, each individually labelled with the tenants' names, to hold their letters, Finch assumed. Telephone directories were ranged below it and a small, black notebook with the word 'Addresses' on the cover lay next to the telephone. Finch moved it to one side as he reached for the receiver and began dialling the number of police headquarters.

Half-way through, he paused. The lift, which must have been on an upper floor, chose that moment to descend, the gates clashing open as a man and woman emerged and crossed the foyer to the main entrance door. The metallic crash was clearly audible even behind the closed window of the cubicle.

Finch flung the receiver back on to its cradle and raced into the foyer where the porter, having opened the door into the street for the departing tenants, was standing on the threshold, staring with a total lack of interest at the line of parked cars outside.

'Tell me,' Finch demanded, jerking his head in the direction of the lodge, 'is that door kept locked?'

'Well, I don't usually bother,' the man admitted. As he spoke, Finch was lugging him by the arm across the foyer. 'Here, steady on!' he protested. 'What's all this in aid of?'

'So anyone could use that phone without you knowing?'

'I suppose so, although I'm usually around keeping an eye on things.'

Finch refrained from mentioning the fact that he certainly hadn't been around, as he described it, when he himself had come down the stairs.

'What's in that book?' he asked, dragging the porter half inside the cubicle.

The man leered at him.

'It's written on the front or can't you read? It's my address book. I keep all the addresses of the residents in there in case letters have to be forwarded. A lot of them have places in the country or abroad.'

'So the address of Mr Bannister's cottage would be in it?'

They were crowded together into the tiny space and Finch had difficulty in getting an arm free to turn the pages.

As the porter answered casually, 'Yes, it's written down in there. He's got a cottage in Suffolk. He often spends his holidays there,' Finch found the entry: Mr H. Bannister, Thatch End, Lambourne, Suffolk.

'Christ!' he said softly.

13

'Christ!' Boyce said. 'Munro? I can't believe it.'

They were in Finch's car, the Sergeant at the wheel, heading east out of London.

In the scramble to get away, Finch had given him only the briefest of accounts. In addition to telephoning the local police station to ask them to hold Hugo Bannister until an escort could be sent from Chelmsford, he had also rung headquarters, not only to inform them of Bannister's arrival but to ask them to keep Munro in the building on some pretext should he happen to turn up. There hadn't been much time for explanation. He had merely told the duty Sergeant to get in touch with Colchester and ask them to send an unmarked car to keep watch on Bannister's cottage at Lambourne with orders to arrest anyone who approached it.

'And tell them to be discreet about it,' Finch had ordered.

Meanwhile Boyce, his face alive with curiosity, had listened in, his head inside the tiny cubicle.

At the last moment, just as they were making for the door, the porter had stopped them.

'Here, what about paying for all those calls?' he demanded.

Finch had flung a five-pound note at him as they ran for the door.

'With any luck we should be there not long after him,' Finch added as they scrambled into the car and Boyce drew away from the kerb. 'He left in the worst of the rush hour and we're only about half an hour behind him. If you could put your foot down . . . '

He left the rest of the sentence unfinished as Boyce forced his way into Marylebone Road under the nose of a bus.

'But what put you on to him?' the Sergeant asked.

'Luck,' Finch said succinctly. 'If that lift hadn't come down just as I was about to phone, I might never have rumbled him.'

'What's the lift got to do with it?'

Finch was about to sigh at Boyce's obtuseness when he realized the Sergeant could not know the significance of the situation.

'Munro phoned me this afternoon to tell me he'd traced the furniture to Hugo Bannister. He said he was calling from the shop and I'd no reason then to doubt him. In the middle of the call, just as he was giving me Bannister's address, there was a clanging noise in the background, like metal being crashed together. He said it was something being delivered. But he was lying, Tom. That noise I heard was the sound of the lift gates at the block of flats where Bannister lives. I recognized it as soon as I heard it. And that made me ask myself why Munro should lie about where he was phoning from and what he was doing at Bannister's address when he told me he was ringing from the shop.'

'So why had he gone there?'

'I'm not sure. I haven't had time yet to work out all the implications myself. But one thing I'm damned sure of: he killed Chivers and Aspinell and he's on his way now, I believe, to murder Benny Costello. Let me start from the beginning, though, and if I say anything that doesn't make sense or seems to have a flaw in the reasoning, just point it out to me, will you?'

'Will do,' Boyce concurred.

'Okay. Munro must have got to know Ray Chivers, at least by sight, when he was attached to the Met.'

'Hang on a minute,' Boyce interrupted. 'He came to us from the Chelsea force. So how did he come to know Chivers who was from Bermondsey?'

'Munro must have served some of his time in the East End,

before moving to Chelsea. Remember when we were discussing the type of weapon which had been used to kill Chivers and Aspinell? He said he'd had some experience of East End criminals and knew of an ex-con in Bermondsey who used to make up coshes. He also told us that when the man died about five years ago, his clients gave him a slap-up funeral. We'll have to check with records, of course, but my bet is Munro was on one of the East End forces at the same time. When he made the remark, I didn't take all that much notice of it, but I think it proves he had first-hand knowledge of the area and that's how I believe he got to know Ray Chivers. Chivers had connections with the East End underworld, even thought the links weren't all that strong until he met Garston. But he was most likely hanging round the fringes before then. Now Munro, who was probably a DC at the time, would have made it his job to get acquainted with the local criminals and their hangers-on. All right so far?'

'Yes, I think so,' Boyce replied. 'I suppose he must have seen Chivers in Chelmsford and recognized him?'

'That's my guess, too. We know from the paper bags Munro himself found in that cardboard box of rubbish that Ray Chivers had been shopping in the town centre at Woolworth's and a men's outfitters. I think Munro spotted him on one of these excursions, got curious to know what he was doing so far from his East End haunts and followed him back to Holly Lodge. It was probably then that he realized Ray was on the run. What else would he be doing, holed up in a back-street house that was due for demolition? But whether or not Munro made the connection with the Hampstead burglary and the murder of PC Flowers at that point, I'm not sure. Munro must have heard about the case though. It was splashed all over the papers and the news bulletins. A dead policeman usually makes headline news.' Finch's voice was bitter as he made this last remark. 'My guess is, though, that he didn't put two and two together straight away. But his intention was the same whatever the final outcome – blackmail. If Chivers was on the run from the police, he'd pay Munro to keep his mouth shut so Munro decided to pay him a little visit on Friday evening.

'What happened can be pieced together from what Hugo Bannister has told us and also from Beach's statement. Bannister called on Ray that evening and took him out for a drink. They got back to the house at about a quarter to eleven. Benny was already there, waiting for Ray – God knows why. We'll find that out from Benny when we pick him up; if we're not too late, that is. I think someone else was also waiting – Munro, watching these comings and goings from his car which was parked somewhere near the house. But somebody saw him.'

'Aspinell?' Boyce suggested.

'Yes. He was coming home from spending the evening at Beach's. We know from Beach that he used Temperance Street as part of his route home to Charlton Road. He'd already mentioned to Beach earlier in the evening that he'd seen a light on in Holly Lodge but, as he didn't mention noticing a car, I think it's safe to assume he saw it on his way home. He certainly spoke of a car later to his son-in-law. Munro drives a dark blue Cortina, doesn't he?'

'That's right.' Boyce sounded abstracted. He was edging the car through the last tangle of traffic in Redbridge. A few minutes later, he joined the M11.

'Thank God, now I can put my foot down,' he added, as, pressing on the accelerator, he moved into the fast lane.

Finch waited until the car had settled down to a steady cruising speed of seventy before picking up the account again.

'We're back to guessing what happened after that, but I think Benny Costello must have left Holly Lodge some time later that evening – about half past eleven I think. Marion Greave said that Chivers had been drinking spirits about an hour before he died. Now that Bannister has told us that he bought Ray Chivers a couple of rum and cokes and they left the pub about half past ten, that would place Chivers' death at roughly half past eleven. Munro saw Costello leave, waited a few minutes until he was clear of the area, and then went up to the house and knocked at the door.'

'And Chivers let him in?' Boyce sounded incredulous.

'He must have done, Tom – God alone knows why. Perhaps

we'll get the answer to that one when we pick up Munro. Anyway, once he was inside the house, he had Chivers where he wanted him. Chivers daren't shout for help; he was being hunted on a murder charge or at least as an accessory. Anyway, supposing he thought of it, no one was likely to hear him. The house is isolated with no immediate neighbours. Munro asked him for money to keep his mouth shut and Ray went upstairs to fetch some of the proceeds from the Hampstead burglary. It may have been then that Munro first made the connection with that particular crime. Or perhaps he frightened Ray into telling him the truth. And that was why he decided to murder him.'

'You've lost me,' Boyce confessed. 'Why should Munro decide to murder Chivers? He could have gone on milking him for weeks.'

'I'm guessing again, Tom, but twenty-five thousand quid in a lump sum is a hell of a temptation. That was the proceeds from the Hampstead job, don't forget. There may have been other reasons: Ray could have gone for him or perhaps he said something to make Munro think he was planning on moving. After all, he couldn't have intended staying in that house indefinitely. All the signs were he was only staying there temporarily.'

'I'll buy that,' Boyce conceded. 'So he smashed Chivers over the head with some sort of cosh he was carrying just in case Chivers turned rough.'

'Not some sort of cosh, Tom – a very special weapon. Remember how Marion Greave described it? Like a small baseball bat.'

Even in the excitement of the moment, as all the pieces began dropping into place, Finch felt a small, self-conscious stir as he spoke her name aloud to the Sergeant. Boyce seemed mercifully unaware of it.

'So?' he asked.

'There's one weapon which fits that description perfectly. I had it at the back of my mind during the investigation. It seemed linked with what Nunn told me about Garston impersonating a uniformed sergeant when Mitchell's safe was burgled.

But I didn't make the connection until now. Think, Tom. What weapon would a policeman have easy access to which fits that description?'

'Bloody hell!' Boyce said admiringly, but whether at his own deductive powers, the Chief Inspector's or Munro's sheer nerve Finch couldn't tell. 'A policeman's truncheon!'

'Exactly. Being smooth, it left no traces in the wound either, of course. No rust particles or splinters of wood. Anyway, to get back to the account. Munro helped himself to the twenty-five thousand quid and cleared off. He'd left no evidence at the scene of the crime, certainly not any prints, which makes me think he must have been wearing gloves.

'And there was only one witness to him having been in the area at all, Stanley Aspinell, although Munro of course didn't know his name at that point. Even so, he must have felt fairly safe. Perhaps the man hadn't seen him or, if he had, wouldn't come forward as a witness. It must have come as a hell of a shock to both of them when they came face to face in the entrance hall at headquarters.'

'So that's why Aspinell cleared off as soon as we arrived!' Boyce exclaimed. 'I wondered why.'

'So did I. But if we accept the fact of Munro's guilt, it makes sense. It must have scared the living daylights out of them both: Aspinell because he realized the man he had seen and whose description he was going to pass on to me was a detective working with me on the murder case; Munro because the man was prepared to make a statement to the police and he now knew his identity. But what Munro didn't know, at least for the time being, was Aspinell's name and address, so there was nothing he could do about it.'

'Which I supplied,' Boyce put in disgustedly. 'Munro was there when I reported back from interviewing Beach.'

'You weren't to know, Tom,' Finch reassured him.

'I know, but all the same . . . ' Boyce fell silent at the enormity of the implications.

Remembering Nunn's words, the Chief Inspector remarked half to himself, 'The rotten apple in the barrel. The trouble is, Tom, that unless you know it's there, it's often the last place you think of looking. Christ!' he added, more violently, 'I feel like smashing him myself!'

'I never liked him,' Boyce offered the comment almost apologetically. 'Too clever by half, that's his trouble. He made me feel . . . ' He broke off as he searched for the right word, unused to expressing his emotions. ' . . . inadequate. I can't explain it. Middle-aged and over the hill.'

Finch took a quick, surreptitious sideways glance at the Sergeant's profile. It looked faintly surprised as if Boyce had startled himself with his own perspicacity. 'Mind you,' he added, 'he was bright. I'll give him that.'

'Oh, yes,' Finch agreed. 'He was intelligent all right. Ruthless, too, although I didn't see how dangerous that side of his personality could be.'

He realized they were both referring to Munro in the past tense as if he no longer existed. Which he'd soon do, Finch thought grimly – at least, as a policeman.

'To get back to the account. He knew Aspinell was away from home that evening,' Finch continued, refraining from pointing out that the man had also acquired that piece of information from Boyce when he had reported back. 'He must have called at the house early the next morning on the off-chance that he was at home. Marion Greave estimated the time of Aspinell's death at about six a.m.'

This time he managed to refer to her with no feeling of self-consciousness.

'Hang on a minute,' Boyce interrupted. 'If Aspinell knew Munro by sight and suspected he was involved in the Temperance Street murder, why the hell did he get out of bed and let him in?'

'It was still fairly dark at that time in the morning,' Finch explained. He had been concerned over this point himself and had given it some consideration. 'It's possible also that Munro managed to borrow a helmet or at least one of those flat uniform caps and was wearing a dark overcoat, rather as Garston did on that Hampstead raid. Someone looking down out of a window would see only the top of a policeman's uniform. It's probable Munro didn't let Aspinell get a good look at his face when he called that morning so the old man wouldn't have been suspicious. After all, Aspinell had been to headquarters himself the previous afternoon. He must have thought we'd traced him and sent someone round to interview him.'

'At six o'clock in the morning!'

'You said yourself Munro was bright. I've no doubt he had some plausible excuse ready. "Sorry to disturb you, sir. Urgent police enquries".'

Finch mimicked the heavy, formal, reassuring voice which policemen are supposed to assume on such occasions.

'With Aspinell dead,' he continued, 'there was only one person left who could be a potential danger to him and that was Benny Costello. And he learnt of Costello's connection with Ray from me, who passed it on from Nunn.' Finch's voice sounded bitter. 'I think Munro's reasoning went like this: he'd seen Ray Chivers in the town centre, but supposing Chivers had seen him? Munro couldn't be sure on that point. And if Chivers had, there was nothing to stop him from saying to Benny, "Remember that copper, Munro, who used to be around the Bermondsey area? Well, I saw him today in Chelmsford." So to be on the safe side, Costello had to be eliminated as well. The only trouble was Benny had gone into hiding and no one knew where he was. It meant, of course, that we couldn't question him which was to Munro's advantage. But Munro had to get to him first if he could. I think that's why he went round to Bannister's place this afternoon.'

'You've lost me,' Boyce admitted.

'Look at it from Munro's point of view,' Finch said. 'He's just found out the name and address of another of Ray Chivers' boyfriends, Hugo Bannister. So before telephoning the information in to me, he decided to go there himself first and try to suss out the situation. But when he got to Bannister's flat, he found there wasn't a lot he could do. At that time, Bannister still hadn't returned from his office. Besides, there was a porter on duty who made it difficult for Munro to do much nosing around. But the porter was also in the habit of nipping down to his basement for a quiet drink. I think Munro took the opportunity to use the phone in his lodge to ring me. He daren't wait too long before putting in the call. I might check at the shop and discover what time Munro had been there and had been given Bannister's address. There was a risk, of course, that I might also discover he hadn't phoned from the shop, but it was a small one and Munro decided to chance his arm. It was his bad luck that the lift gates happened to open just as he was in the middle of the call to me so that later I was able to realize he'd been lying. But, at the time, Munro thought up an excuse which seemed to satisfy me and he probably thought he'd got away with it. But he also had a bit of good luck at the same time. He noticed the address book lying by the phone in which the porter had written down all the holiday addresses of the tenants in case mail had to be forwarded to them. Munro checked on Bannister's name and found he had a cottage in Suffolk. It must have seemed to him possible that Benny Costello could be holed up there. After all, the three men were connected: Ray Chivers, Hugo Bannister and Benny himself. Anyway, as far as Munro was concerned, it was worth checking out. And, God Almighty, I gave him half an hour's start on us!'

'I thought he didn't seem all that disappointed when you picked me to be in on the interview with Bannister,' Boyce put in, not very tactfully.

'So did I, but I didn't give it a second thought.'

'Well, perhaps they're holding him at headquarters.' Boyce tried to sound hopeful.

'If he went there,' Finch replied, 'which I doubt. Don't forget, I told him to push off home. Christ,' he continued in an angry outburst, 'he must have been laughing up his sleeve all the bloody time! That's what gets up my nose. He was in on the inquiries, he knew every move we made at the time we made it. He even helped with the investigation. He must have thought he was sitting pretty, especially when we were convinced it was Garston who had committed the murders.'

Boyce had the sense to keep silent for once. There was no point in rubbing salt into the wounds.

They had reached the end of the motorway some time before and had slowed down as they turned off the A12 towards Dedham.

It was now completely dark and the headlamps cut swathes of light in front of them, illuminating the narrow country roads, grass verges and the bare branches of trees on which a few leaves, like ragged flags left over from some long-ago celebration, still clung. Isolated villages loomed up briefly in a scatter of lights and then fell back again as darkened countryside reasserted itself. There was no moon; the sky was too overcast for it to be visible, although the landscape showed up dimly against the horizon in gently rounded contours.

They were in Suffolk and Finch was surprised, as he always was, by the changed shape of the countryside. Only a few miles away across the Stour, Essex lay flat and monotonous, laid out in fields of sugar-beet and winter barley. Although he personally liked the landscape with its long vistas and wide skies, he could see that it could hardly be described as picturesque.

Suffolk began on the other side of the river where the land suddenly lifted and the trees crowded closer together. Here was rural England as the tourists knew it from the postcards and illustrated brochures: thatched cottages and pretty timbered villages and those huge churches whose spires and towers dominated the view, built in the county's prosperous past when the wool-merchants celebrated their wealth in flint and stone and thanked God for their riches in carved wood and stained glass.

They must soon be nearing the village of Lambourne, Finch thought, although in the tangle of lanes and by-roads it was difficult to choose a direct route. To make matters more difficult, they had no map of the area with them and, on several occasions, Boyce had to stop the car and get out to read a signpost which, stuck on a grass verge in the middle of nowhere, pointed its arms in three or four directions at some tiny road junction.

Finch waited in the car, seething with impatience. Not that it was Boyce's fault. There was not even anyone from whom to ask directions: not a house nor even a farm. The men who tilled these fields were scattered thinly across them.

On the third occasion, Boyce climbed back into the driver's seat and announced, 'Found the bloody place at last! It's down here.'

Turning the car to the right, he set off down a road so narrow that in places the branches of the trees met across it.

Lambourne itself was nothing more than a tiny huddle of houses and cottages: no church although it had a pub and a village shop. As they passed through it, Finch noticed the telephone kiosk from which Bannister had intended calling the police before changing his mind.

They saw the police car parked about a quarter of a mile the other side of the village, drawn up in a gateway with its lights off. As Boyce pulled in behind it, Finch got out and approached the driver's window.

'I'm Detective Chief Inspector Finch,' he announced, showing the uniformed man behind the wheel his official identification. As he spoke, he tried to hide his anger.

He'd said an unmarked car, for God's sake, and yet there they were – two uniformed men sitting inside a vehicle with the bloody word 'Police' stuck on the side for anyone to see. Someone had made a balls-up and that person, he thought grimly, would pay for it. He'd kick his backside in for him personally.

'Seen anything?' he asked. 'Has any car passed you?'

'No, nothing, sir,' the driver replied. 'And we've been here for the best part of an hour.'

'Where's the cottage?'

The driver pointed straight ahead at the windscreen.

'It's about ten minutes' walk further down the lane.'

'Are there any houses nearby?'

'No, it stands on its own.'

'Right,' Finch said. 'I want you two to come with me. We may be going to make an arrest and it could be tricky, so watch out for yourselves.'

There wasn't any time to explain the situation in any detail. Even that brief warning seemed to Finch to take up too much time. He still felt keyed-up by an overwhelming sense of urgency, even though the presence of the police car had quietened some of his fears.

Having turned off the car engine and the lights, Boyce joined them in the road.

'I want a quiet approach,' Finch continued. 'No talking and keep to the verge. I don't want our approach heralded by the tramp of feet.' Turning to Boyce, he added, 'You keep with me, Tom. You other two, stay in the background as back-up in case anything goes wrong. If it does, use your initiative.'

'Very good, sir,' the two men replied in chorus.

Finch peered at them through the darkness. They looked solid enough, their bulk outlined against the gate opening. He could only hope to God their heads weren't as thick as their shoulders.

Looking up at the sky, he was thankful it wasn't raining; he could have done with a little more light though. The night was thick and muffled although he comforted himself with the thought that, if Munro turned up, he'd find the darkness as much to his disadvantage as it was to theirs.

They set off in single file, Finch leading the way, treading softly along the grass verge. Like bloody Red Indians, the Chief Inspector thought with sour humour. Well, there was one particular scalp it'd give him great pleasure to hang on his belt.

The cottage was on their left, set back from the road behind hedges. A white-painted gate led into a gravelled driveway, which glimmered dimly like a pale stream, leading up to the front door before branching off behind the cottage, probably to a garage out of sight behind the building. Finch cursed under his breath. On such a surface, their approach was hardly going to be silent.

Lights were on in the cottage, two in the downstairs windows, one on the first floor. Their presence was reassuring. The place looked normal, comforting almost; and Finch remembered homecomings of his childhood when he had walked up to the door of his own country home into the warmth and dazzle of his mother's kitchen, the kettle boiling on the stove and the smell of newly ironed linen.

Boyce's voice cut into his brief reverie.

'Oh, Christ, look!'

He was pointing further up the lane and, for a moment, Finch couldn't make out what he had seen. Then, as he adjusted his eyes to the distance, he saw it for himself.

The car was parked close to the hedge and appeared, at first glance, to form part of its bulk. Boyce, who had run forward, turned to Finch who was following on his heels.

'It's Munro's,' he announced, although Finch had already guessed that for himself. He added, 'The engine's still warm. He can't have arrived all that long ago.'

'Too bloody long,' Finch said bitterly. As the Sergeant spoke, he had grasped the situation. The road sloped downwards. Munro had simply approached the cottage from the opposite direction to the village, turning off his lights and engine and coasting down the hill.

He couldn't have known the police car was on watch. He must have taken the precaution in order that Benny wouldn't be warned of his arrival.

'Come on!' Finch shouted.

Silence was no longer important and, as he pounded up the gravel drive, the small stones scattering under his feet, the lights he could see in the cottage no longer signified safety and reassurance but seemed to be signals of disaster.

14

Benny was bored. Despite his assurances to Hugo that, unlike Ray, he enjoyed the countryside, the cottage and its surroundings gave him the creeps. It was mainly the silence. It seemed to gather like a palpable weight that he could feel pressing in on him until he could imagine it as a huge, dark hand between his shoulder blades.

In contrast, the sudden and unexpected noises were terrifyingly loud: the scuttle of a bird through the bushes, the creak of branch against branch, the dry, sibilant whisper of dead leaves and grasses.

It was worse after dark. As the light faded, the house itself seemed to take on life, its beams and timbers creaking and exploding as they stretched into a weird existence of their own as if they had taken root again after all those centuries. It was then that he noticed the wind which seemed to wake at dusk and come pouring over the roof in a black tide like rushing water until at times he was afraid it would engulf the cottage and sweep it and himself away in a great vortex of oblivion.

And the darkness! Benny had never known nights to be so dark. There was nothing to pierce it, neither street lamps nor even a moon nor stars. Even the cottage lights, which he turned on as soon as twilight began to threaten, seemed too puny to illuminate anything except their small, immediate centres. Beyond them, the shadows collected in the corners of the rooms while, outside the cottage, he was aware of the blackness crowding up close against the windows behind the drawn curtains.

His only consolation was the whisky which Hugo had left him and, as each day passed, he began drinking earlier until by nightfall he was far from sober and by bed-time he was sufficiently drunk for the sharp edges of his fears to be blunted and he could sleep.

In the daytime, he occupied himself as best he could. There were logs to be brought in from the garage where they were stacked against the back wall and kindling to be found. A small pile of chopped wood had also been left in the garage and, when that ran out, he broke branches from the trees to take indoors for the fire. He hated lighting it. The wood never seemed to catch the first time, subsiding into a smouldering mound of blackened logs. Coughing and cursing, Benny had to rake the whole bloody lot out on to the hearth and start again.

He also explored the garden, prowling round its perimeter and kicking moodily at the grass. Behind the garage he found a gap in the hedge which surrounded the garden and walked through it to the field beyond but there was nothing to see, only ploughed earth, grey sky and a distant clump of trees round which rooks circled. Even at that distance, he could hear their bad-tempered cries.

No one called at the cottage and for that, at least, he was grateful. Its isolation seemed to make it safe from Garston and his friends. It was the last place they'd come looking for him.

All the same, whenever a car went along the lane, Benny held himself rigid, listening, until it had passed.

He was totally unprepared for the knock on the door on Friday evening. He was standing in the kitchen at the time, the lid of the deep-freeze open as he searched through the packets and plastic bags, stiff and opaque with frost, for something to cook for his supper.

It would have to bloody lamb chops again, he thought. But at least they were easy.

It was then that the knocking came.

Benny straightened up. Shock and fright cleared his mind of the effects of the whisky he had drunk earlier, although he was still aware that he had less control over his limbs.

As he lowered the lid slowly and silently, his thoughts rushed ahead, assessing the situation.

The lights were on upstairs and down. There was no chance, therefore, that the caller would go away, thinking the cottage was empty. Thank Christ the curtains were drawn! The front door was locked but the back door was unfastened and, stepping soundlessly across the kitchen, Benny slid the top and bottom bolts into position.

A small, rational part of his mind told him that possibly all these precautions could be unnecessary. The caller might be some casual visitor from the village, quite harmless. But he scarcely listened. A stronger and more intuitive process, the instinct for self-preservation, warned him otherwise.

No way, he told himself. It was Garston or one of his friends. The very knocking itself seemed to foretell death.

A weapon! he thought. There was a poker in the sitting-room, but not much else in the house he could use if the man broke in. And, knowing Garston, that wouldn't be much use to him. He might be carrying a shooter. Besides, if it came to a rough house, he knew he wouldn't stand a chance and Christ! he didn't want to finish up like Ray with the side of his head bashed in.

Flight seemed the best solution but where would he run to and how the hell could he get out of the cottage in time?

He had to stall the man somehow; make him think that he'd

open the door eventually, thus giving himself time to make a getaway.

Walking lightly, Benny crossed the sitting-room and went up the stairs, horribly conscious of the man's presence just a few feet away on the other side of the front door. He mounted cautiously, taking his weight off the treads so that they wouldn't creak by placing his hands against the walls. At the top, he turned into the front bedroom which was Hugo's and, taking a blanket from the bed, flung it round his shoulders. At a pinch, he thought, it'd look like a towel.

Opening the window, he stuck his head out.

'Who is it?' he called.

It was too dark to see the man clearly. All Benny could distinguish was a foreshortened figure standing below at the front door although a pale blur of a face was tipped up towards the window.

'Mr Costello?' the man asked.

So he knew his name, Benny thought. As he had feared, the man was no casual visitor.

Trying to keep his voice normal, Benny replied, 'Yes, I am. What do you want? Only I've just got out of the bath.'

'I'd like a few words with you if you can spare a moment.'

It wasn't Garston, Benny realized. The man's voice, politely pleasant, was unknown to him.

'What about?' Benny demanded.

'It's about Ray. I know something that could be of help to you.'

Frigging liar! Benny thought. The only help you're going to give me, mate, is at the end of a bloody iron bar.

'Oh, right!' Benny made his voice sound eagerly grateful. 'If you can hang on for a minute, I'll get a dressing gown and come down to let you in.'

The man nodded – at least, the pale shape below the window moved and then disappeared as the man's head tipped down again. From his stance, Benny guessed he was standing relaxed at the door, waiting for it to be opened.

Benny reckoned he had about two or three minutes before the man became suspicious – not long but at least a start.

Flinging the blanket down on the bed, he moved quickly out of the room and into his own which overlooked the back garden.

On the first morning he had wakened in the cottage, he had noticed the long cat's-slide roof below the window which stretched down to within a few feet of the ground. At the time, he hadn't paid much attention to it except as an unusual feature of the building. Now he thanked Christ it was there; it was to be his escape route.

Opening the window silently, he peered down its long slope into the darkness. He couldn't see much. He had turned the light off as he had entered the room and he daren't turn it on again, not even for a moment.

The thatch was covered with fine wire meshing; to keep the birds out, he assumed, and, as he put his hands down, he could feel it.

There was no frigging chance, therefore, of sliding down the thatch. The sodding netting would catch on his clothes. He'd have to let himself down slowly.

As he climbed on to the sill and manoeuvred himself backwards through the tiny opening, he wished to God he hadn't drunk so much bloody whisky. His hands were trembling and his legs, as he lowered them down the slope, felt like putty. His head was swimming, too, although he realized that this was as much the thought of the emptiness below him, even though he couldn't see it in the darkness, as the effects of the booze.

But there was no other way out.

Here we bloody go! he thought as, fingers scrambling for a hold on the netting, he swung himself off the sill.

The down-draught from the roof caught him by surprise as it buffeted against his body, making him lose his grip. The slope was steeper, too, than he had thought and its angle, pulling with the weight of his body, dragged him downwards.

He felt himself slithering out of control, the sharp snags on the netting catching at his hands and clothes. Even so, time seemed to be suspended and it appeared to him that the downward rush went on for several agonizing minutes in which his mind, despite its terror, was able to go on working with a suspended clarity, as it does sometimes in dreams, so that it seemed unconnected with the rest of his body.

His first thought was that the man must have heard him. The noise seemed deafening to him – the ripping of fabric, the metallic, shirring noise as he slid over the netting and, below that, the creak and rustle of the thatch under his weight.

But this fear was soon superseded by another – the terror of falling. There was a flagged patio below. If he hit that, he wouldn't have a chance in hell. At worst, he could break a leg and, even if he got away with just a sprained ankle, he'd be in no state to make a run for it.

He felt his feet drop over the bottom edge of the thatch and, scrambling frantically with his fingers, clutched at the netting, hooking them into the mesh.

Blood ran warm over his hands but he was not aware of any pain, only relief as he felt his body slow down. He let himself hang for several seconds, legs swinging free, as he recovered his breath, before inching himself down the last few feet of the roof until he could let himself drop on to the flagstones.

All the same, he landed more awkwardly than he had intended, his feet thudding down on to the hard surface.

Without waiting to discover if the man had heard him, he was off, running across the dark garden towards the garage and the gap in the hedge.

Behind him he could hear feet pounding along the gravel and a shout as the man gave chase.

He had, Benny reckoned, a minute's start: not long enough but, at least, he knew where the gap was and, as he broke through it into the field and made off across it towards the clump of trees on the far side, he could hear the man cursing as he fumbled his way round the side of the garage.

He had only gone a few yards when Benny realized his mistake. The earth was ploughed up into ridges and was soaking wet with the recent rain. Within seconds his shoes were clogged with mud, making it impossible for him to run fast. For the first time, too, he was aware of the pain in his hands and he sucked his fingers before tucking them into his armpits to ease them, tasting the blood warm and salty in his mouth. His chest hurt as well and he could feel his heart banging against his ribs as if trying to batter its way out.

It's like a bloody nightmare, he thought, and heard himself begin to whimper, a low, keening sound which came bubbling up out of his throat without any conscious effort on his part.

Boyce shouldered the front door of the cottage open, throwing his weight against it. It crashed back, the jamb splintered round the lock and bolts.

So much for security, Finch thought grimly, as he followed Boyce into the tiny hall.

'You search the downstairs!' he shouted, taking the stairs two at a time.

The front bedroom was empty, its light on and a blanket slung down on the bed, but the back bedroom was in darkness and, as Finch entered and flicked on the switch, he saw the open window and guessed what had happened. Sticking his head briefly through it, he looked down the long slope of the roof before clattering back down the stairs.

'Nothing down here,' Boyce reported, meeting him at the foot of the staircase.

'No, he's made off down the roof,' Finch told him.

The two uniformed men had meanwhile crowded into the hall with them and, as Finch shoved them back, he demanded, 'Have either of you got a torch?'

If they say no, I'll bloody blow my top, he thought furiously.

'I have, sir,' one of them replied, flourishing it.

Finch seized it.

'Now, listen,' he said rapidly. 'I want you two to search the front. Cover the road but not into the village. No one passed us on the way here so, if they've made off, it'll be in the opposite direction. You, Tom, come with me. We'll search behind the cottage. If anyone sees or hears anything, give a shout. Understood?'

'We're looking for two men, are we, sir?' one of the uniformed men asked.

Finch almost lost his temper and then realized that neither of them knew what was happening.

'Yes, two,' he replied. 'And one will be chasing the other, so you can't mistake them.' It was a cheap piece of sarcasm which he regretted but at least it relieved some of his feelings. 'And I want both of them caught before one of them gets killed.'

Without waiting to see their reaction, he bundled Boyce out of the front door, switching on the torch as he did so.

It had a powerful beam and lit up the gravelled drive as they ran along it. At the end, where it opened up on to a hard stand in front of the garage, he swung it round to illuminate the garden, noting the high hedges.

Boyce, who had stopped to test the garage door, called out, 'Nothing here. The door's locked.'

'But they must have made off through the garden,' Finch said, half to himself, swinging the torch round so that it lit up the long slope of the back roof.

It seemed the only logical route for Benny to take. He'd be in a panic, of course but, even so, he wouldn't have run round to the front of the house where the man must have been waiting. Otherwise, Benny would have escaped through the front door and he hadn't done that; it had been bolted. Besides, the open window could only mean he'd cleared off down the roof.

And yet the garden seemed totally enclosed and there was no sign, as he swung the torch round again, of any break in the hedge where someone had broken through.

It was Boyce who supplied the answer. He had fumbled his way round the side of the garage and now, raising his voice, shouted, 'There's a gap in the hedge here!'

They squeezed through it and stood on the edge of the field: ploughland, Finch noted with disgust, as he ran the beam of the torch over the furrows. And bloody well wet through into the bargain. Although powerful, the torch wasn't strong enough to penetrate more than a few yards into the darkness and there was no noise that Finch could hear, even though he strained to listen, apart from the usual night noises: the wind in the trees, the faint rustle of some creature in the hedge bottom and the tiny, less definable sounds which the coutryside produces after nightfall and which, taken together, make up a huge background of silence.

If only it wasn't so bloody dark! Finch thought savagely.

As if in answer, the clouds drifted apart, revealing a dim moon swimming in milky light and a few moist stars.

'Thank God!' Finch said out loud.

The light wasn't much. Under normal circumstances, he wouldn't have thought of it as moonlight at all, only a thinner darkness, but at least there was enough of it to bring the far side of the field into sight and the outlines of bare trees against the sky.

And something else: a figure emerging from them to the left, briefly silhouetted, before it plunged out of sight behind the brow of the hill.

Benny reached the trees, scrambling through a ditch into the safety of their closeness.

He could hide, he thought. If he kept perfectly still, he wouldn't be found. It was too bloody dark for his pursuer to pick him out from among the tree trunks and bushes. Although what the hell he did when daylight came, he had no idea.

Get further in, he told himself and crashed through the undercover of thicket.

It was then that the sodding moon broke through the clouds.

He turned his face up towards it as it hung above the stripped branches and let fly with a stream of obscenities.

It was no good now hoping to hide. His best bet was to break cover and make off across the fields. Surely to God he'd find a cottage or a farmhouse somewhere?

He emerged from the trees and paused momentarily. Behind him, the crackle of twigs underfoot told him that his pursuer was only minutes away.

Benny looked about him, assessing his surroundings. At least, there was now enough light to pick out details of the landscape. He realized he was on top of rising ground which sloped away behind the wood. Below, in the distance, he could see the faint gleam of a river and lights shining.

A village! he thought jubilantly. Christ, he was saved.

The pain in his hands and chest no longer seemed to matter and, swinging his arms free, he set off at a run down the slope.

Finch and Boyce ran diagonally across the ploughed field towards the point where they had seen the figure disappear. As they ran, Finch saw a second figure emerge from the trees and dip out of sight.

'Munro!' he called back over his shoulder.

Boyce merely grunted. Since giving a shout to warn the uniformed men before he and Finch set off across the field, he had said nothing apart from cursing under his breath but even that had stopped as he concentrated his strength on keeping going over the uneven ground.

There had been an answering shout from the direction of the road, but Finch did not hold out much hope of the two men catching up with them in time to be much help. They had no torch and it was unlikely they'd find the gap in the hedge. They'd waste minutes trying to break through it.

He and Boyce reached the far side of the ploughed field where they paused briefly to scrape the heavy mud from their shoes on the long grass before clambering through a ditch and over a fence into the next meadow.

It was pasture, thank God, Finch thought. The going would be easier.

He could no longer make out the two figures; they had merged into the background of trees and bushes which grew more densely here along the edges of the fields, but he could guess where Benny would be heading for: the lights at the bottom of the hill.

As they ran down the sloping meadow, their feet slithering on the wet grass, Finch orientated himself.

The river was the Stour. Over to his right, therefore, where there was a more distant but denser cluster of lights, would be Dedham. The closer, looser sprinkling of lights must be from the group of houses and cottages round Flatford Mill.

He had been there several times with his sister, who liked Constable country, and he tried to remember its layout as he ran towards it. There was the mill itself, of course, which was now a Field Centre, and close by, near the bridge, a thatched cottage which sold postcards and tourists' mementoes and where, in summer, you could get tea in a small garden and hire boats to row up the river. Further off were more houses including Willy Lott's cottage, but he couldn't recall their exact positions in relation to the mill or the bridge.

As for the rest, there was a car-park and, over the bridge, flat, lush water-meadows and willow trees along the bank.

In summer, the place was crowded with visitors but on a late October night there'd be nobody there although the lights suggested that some of the houses, if not the Field Centre itself, must be occupied.

If only Benny could get there before Munro caught up with him he'd be safe.

Benny reached the bottom of the hill and paused. As he descended, the vista had shifted and he no longer had the same clear view of the lights as he had had from the top of the slope. It was confusing. They had seemed closer together and much more visible. Now they were scattered and partly hidden behind the surrounding trees.

But at least he had reached a road and, clambering over a gate, he ran down it towards the houses.

A cottage came into view, standing beside a bridge, but its front windows were in darkness. Behind it, lights shone out on to water. He could see their reflections lengthened and trembling on its surface.

They were on the other side of the bridge, he told himself, and ran across it.

As he reached the further bank, he realized he had made his second and greater mistake. It had been a trick of his angle of vision. The lights weren't on the far side. They were on the nearer bank after all and the river now lay between him and them.

There was not time to turn back. As he reached the end of the bridge and stepped on to a raised, grassy path which ran along the riverbank, he heard his pursuer's feet clatter on to it at the far side. There was nothing he could do except keep running towards the lights.

But I can't swim! he thought. Christ, what do I do?

The sense of nightmare closed in on him again and he sobbed out loud, feeling the tears run down his face.

Like a frigging kid, he told himself. For God's sake, you can sodding well shout, can't you?

The words seemed to come from somewhere quite separate from himself: a hard, cold, contemptuous voice which shocked him out of his panic and released his real voice.

Yelling, he pounded along the path towards the lights on the far side of the river.

Finch heard the shouts and thought, Oh, God, we're too late!

They had reached the road and, as they ran along it, he had a confused mental image of a raised arm swinging down, a figure slumping to the ground and Munro running off into the darkness.

We'll get him eventually, Finch promised himself viciously.

But the shouts continued. Lights sprang up in the front window of the thatched cottage as they passed and, as Finch yelled back, he realized Benny had crossed the bridge to the far side.

The poor, stupid, little sod! he thought.

The answering shouts brought Benny to a standstill. They also triggered off a reaction which astonished even himself.

Turning, he faced his pursuer.

'You bloody well did for Ray!' he shouted and lunged at him.

The violence of the attack caught them both off balance. Clinging together, they fell down the slope of the banked path and, plunging into the mill-pond, hit the water, scattering the reflections into a thousand tiny pieces of broken light.

'Oh, bloody hell!' Finch said out loud, stripping off his coat as he ran towards them. Behind him, he could hear Boyce also swearing as he did the same.

'You take Munro!' Finch shouted, kicking off his shoes. 'I'll deal with Benny.'

They entered the water together and struck out side by side for the two struggling figures.

Benny was still shouting or attempting to. As he swam

toward him, Finch could see he was in a blind panic, his mouth still open as his head disappeared below water. Munro had him by the legs and, as he shouldered him out of the way, Finch grabbed Benny by the hair, jerking his head upwards and striking him across the chin with his fist at the same time.

I only hope to God I haven't broken his jaw, Finch thought, as, turning the unconscious body on its back and seizing it under the shoulders, he kicked out for the bank. But at least that's better than a smashed skull.

Boyce, who was still in the water, seemed to be having trouble with Munro. The man fought desperately and Finch got to his feet in readiness to dive in again when he saw Boyce's lifted arm crash down on the back of the man's head.

He watched it fall with a sense of *déjà vu*. It was, he realized, a shift into reality of his own mental picture of Munro's attack on Benny and there seemed a dreadful justice in it. It was right, too, that the Sergeant had struck the blow rather than himself. Boyce owed Munro one, he thought, and their account was now settled.

Boyce seemed to be aware of it himself as he dragged Munro up the bank.

'Out cold,' he announced with satisfaction, grinning up at Finch, the water pouring from his clothes and hair.

The two uniformed men arrived shortly afterwards, too late to do much although their presence proved useful. Finch sent one of them off to the Field Centre to telephone for ambulances and extra police reinforcements and, when the man returned, the four of them carried the two unconscious men to the far side of the bridge. Here they were covered with blankets lent by the local residents who had been drawn out of their houses by the noise and excitement, to await the arrival of the ambulances.

Someone made tea. Finch drank his gratefully, his teeth chattering on the rim of the mug.

Physically, he felt chilled to the very bones, but emotionally he was warm and buoyed up. Munro, that rotten apple, was rooted out and Costello was still alive, thank God.

There were still a lot of loose ends to tie up: statements to be taken, not least from Hugo Bannister who must have arrived by this time at headquarters in Chelmsford where he would be waiting for the Chief Inspector's return. God knows what would happen to him. The papers would have to be sent to the DPP and Finch was grateful that the decision regarding his fate was out of his hands. But even if no prosecution was brought against him, he would almost certainly be ruined. The Civil Service, that most conservative of institutions, would no doubt, in the face of the scandal, regard him as another rotten apple to be discarded.

But Finch's mind was concentrated mostly on a problem of his own. The case was virtually over. Two murders had been solved: not a bad record when everything was considered. And in the solving of them, Marion Greave had won her point: both victims had been killed by the same person wielding the same weapon.

Of course, he would have to keep to his promise and take her out to dinner. He couldn't go back on his word.

And after that?

God alone knew.

SUSPICIOUS DEATH

DOROTHY SIMPSON

ACCIDENT, SUICIDE ... OR MURDER?

The woman in the blue sequinned cocktail dress was dragged from her watery grave beneath a bridge. A highly suspicious death – and Inspector Thanet is called in to investigate.

The more he learns about the late Marcia Salden, mistress of Telford Green Manor, the less likely a candidate she seemed for suicide. A successful self-made woman with a thriving business, she had everything she wanted, including the mansion she had coveted since childhood. She also had a knack for stirring up trouble . . .

As Inspector Thanet attempts to unravel the complex sequence of events surrounding her death, he discovers that if Mrs Salden hadn't managed to get herself murdered, it wasn't for want of trying . . .

Also by Dorothy Simpson in Sphere Books:
ELEMENT OF DOUBT
DEAD ON ARRIVAL
LAST SEEN ALIVE
CLOSE HER EYES
PUPPET FOR A CORPSE

0 7474 0128 4   CRIME   £2.99

A selection of bestsellers from SPHERE

FICTION

WILDTRACK	Bernard Cornwell	£3.50 ☐
THE FIREBRAND	Marion Zimmer Bradley	£3.99 ☐
STARK	Ben Elton	£3.50 ☐
LORDS OF THE AIR	Graham Masterton	£3.99 ☐
THE PALACE	Paul Erdman	£3.50 ☐

FILM AND TV TIE-IN

WILLOW	Wayland Drew	£2.99 ☐
BUSTER	Colin Shindler	£2.99 ☐
COMING TOGETHER	Alexandra Hine	£2.99 ☐
RUN FOR YOUR LIFE	Stuart Collins	£2.99 ☐
BLACK FOREST CLINIC	Peter Heim	£2.99 ☐

NON-FICTION

CHAOS	James Gleick	£5.99 ☐
THE SAFE TAN BOOK	Dr Anthony Harris	£2.99 ☐
IN FOR A PENNY	Jonathan Mantle	£3.50 ☐
DETOUR	Cheryl Crane	£3.99 ☐
MARLON BRANDO	David Shipman	£3.50 ☐

All Sphere books are available at your local bookshop or newsagent, or can be ordered direct from the publisher. Just tick the titles you want and fill in the form below.

Name _____

Address _____

_____

Write to Sphere Books, Cash Sales Department, P.O. Box 11, Falmouth, Cornwall TR10 9EN
Please enclose a cheque or postal order to the value of the cover price plus:
UK: 60p for the first book, 25p for the second book and 15p for each additional book ordered to a maximum charge of £1.90.
OVERSEAS & EIRE: £1.25 for the first book, 75p for the second book and 28p for each subsequent title ordered.
BFPO: 60p for the first book, 25p for the second book plus 15p per copy for the next 7 books, thereafter 9p per book.
Sphere Books reserve the right to show new retail prices on covers which may differ from those previously advertised in the text elsewhere, and to increase postal rates in accordance with the P.O.